The Dragons of Zimzor

Written and Illustrated by
Mary Harrison

Mary Harrison

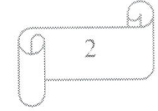

This book and its illustrations have been a journey – a journey dedicated to the inspiration of young readers; those who love a great adventure but not necessarily the act of reading. May this work inspire you to read on and on and on…..

My deepest thanks to my children, students and fellow educators who have given of their time to model the characters within these pages:

Jon-Mark as Eli
Will as Kane

Supporting Characters modeled by:
Barbara, Haley, Joshua, Jessie, Jenna, Kyle, Michelle, R.D., Tate, and Taylor

Mary Harrison

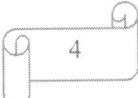

Contents

"And you shall know the truth, and the truth shall make you free."
John 8:32

Mary Harrison

Chapter 1

Eli

Fifteen year old Eli sat in fourth hour science class. The room was hot and stuffy. Eli pushed his sandy blonde hair, limp from the day's humidity, across his tanned forehead and away from his piercing blue eyes. Zimzor's twin suns sent their full rays of midday streaming through the classroom window on his left adding to the interior temperature. Despite his discomfort, Eli leaned forward and concentrated hard on Mr. Elliot's lecture as he described the methods of cross-pollination used by Zimley's agricultural research

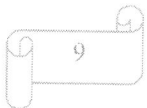

department to enhance corn production.

A firm knock at the classroom door snapped Eli's thoughts away from pollen grains and jerked several sleepy students back into an upright position. The door opened and in walked the principal, Miss Hawkins. She barely glanced at Mr. Elliot before announcing, "I have come for the Harcourt boy."

Eli's heart thundered in his chest while several boys in the back jeered, "Eli's in for it now!"

Stanley, Eli's lab partner, leaned over and whispered, "What'd you do?"

Eli knew better than to keep the principal waiting, so he stood on trembling legs, shrugged and shook his head slightly at Stan, all the while wondering what "The Hawk," that all seeing and ever critical principal, could possibly want with him. Even though he was tall and thin for his age, Eli always felt like a tiny ant in the imposing presence of Miss Hawkins. In meek silence Eli followed her from class, down the hall, past the school office and out the front door.

Much to his dismay, Miss Hawkins did not have a lecture about behavior, truthfulness, or becoming the best person he could be in store for him, but merely gestured for Eli to follow a group of very distinguished men from the town's high council offices. One of the men offered his hand to Eli, who shook it somewhat robotically. Together the group headed across the school lawn, toward the ornate town square and the great governmental building, the largest and most grand edifice in all of Zimley, with a very confused Eli in tow.

Electric excitement filled the air as Eli was ushered into the high council chambers. He recognized the ruling members of Zimley's high council seated before him. Eli scanned the room wondering what could be the purpose of his being in these highly honored chambers where all the most important decrees that governed the land were written. To his great surprise, Eli saw his parents and sister, Marina, seated to the high council's right, as if they, too, were now members of this auspicious inner circle of Zimley's elite. Master Oliver, Zimley's council leader, smiled as he directed Eli to a seat facing the long, ebony table.

"Perhaps you wonder why we have summoned you here, Eli." Oliver paused to clear his throat. "Today we have a very important announcement to make and we wanted you to be the first to hear it!"

Confusion swept over him again as Eli attempted to make sense of the mayor's statement. What could possibly warrant him, a mere fifteen-

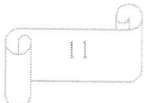

11

year-old student, being the first to hear any high council decree, no matter how small a declaration?

"Do you know what year it is, young man? No, no, I don't mean the date. Not that year," Oliver chuckled. He had seen the quizzical look cross Eli's face at that seemingly ridiculous question. "This is the year when the council must select a new dragon-keeper."

Eli's heart skipped a beat and lump formed in his throat. *It's me, it has to be me.* He repeated the words over in his mind. Eli had secretly wished to become a dragon-keeper ever since he had heard of the dragons as a tiny child not even old enough to attend school. But then so had every other boy his age. All of Eli's best friends at school talked of nothing else these days. He could not remember when they had begun playing games at recess and on holiday breaks, each pretending to be the most gifted of all dragon-keepers. The children always delighted in seeing the mighty dragons fly over town – peaceful protectors of Zimley.

It has to be me. Eli had never actually told his parents how deep and heartfelt was his desire to become a dragon-keeper. He'd always thought they would just laugh. His mind raced and the room seemed vague and distant as Master Oliver read from his proclamation.

"...and each new apprentice must be between thirteen and fifteen years in age. The apprentice must show exceptional qualities of caring, love and willingness to sacrifice for others. Gentleness, kindness and teach-ability are also sought-after qualities. Above all, each dragon-keeper must exhibit truthfulness and integrity under all circumstances."

Eli's attention riveted back and his heart sank at the same time. He feared he was not nearly kind enough and he could not remember a time when he had sacrificed for another. Surely the choice would not be him.

Oliver continued to read, "In addition, our dragon-keeper this year has demonstrated from his earliest days a keen and deep desire to learn about and serve the dragon colony." Master Oliver stopped reading and looked directly into Eli's eyes. "We've been watching you for a long time my young friend. The council has long noticed the way you are always watching the dragons overhead, straining to see their mighty wings flying over the sea every time your family is at the beach. Not only that, Eli, but all your teachers comment on your kindness in class, your joyful attitude and helpfulness to other students. Oh, yes. You possess all the qualities we look for in our young apprentices. You are destined to become a great dragon-keeper someday."

Eli sat perfectly still, numb with disbelief. How could the council have known his deepest desire? *Perhaps my parents petitioned one of the leaders on my behalf.* No, that was not even a possible idea. Eli didn't know which of the council members were involved in the selection process. No one did. That was the best kept secret of Zimley.

"Eli, the council has chosen you to become our newest dragon-keeper."

In his dazed excitement mixed with disbelief, Eli became aware of his father slapping him on the back while saying how proud he was. Meanwhile, his sister, Marina, hopped from her place behind the table and nearly squeezed the breath from him in a giant hug while his mother wiped tears from her eyes.

"Now," Oliver declared, "I do believe that everyone should be assembled in the square if our officers have done their job well. This way please, it is time to read the proclamation to the people."

The Zimley town bells rang out clearly, calling all citizens to the great town square. There was a jovial atmosphere in the crowd as all the Zimleys found a place to stand or sit in the enormous square. Eli thought he might collapse before the Oliver finished his speech. But at long last he did, then cleared his throat and smiled out at the gathered crowd of citizens.

"It gives me great pleasure to present your

new dragon-keeper, Eli Harcourt!"

Eli was led to the platform while the crowd around him cheered. Through the cheering, Eli heard his friends from school take up the chant, "Eli, Eli, Eli…"

Oliver spoke again. "Now Eli, we all congratulate you on being selected to become a dragon-keeper. But we never force this position on anyone. You now have a choice to make. Before you do, however, I must spell out the changes in your life that will take place if you accept this position."

Eli listened intently as Master Oliver explained in detail how he would no longer attend school, for he had more important things to learn. Neither would Eli continue to live with his family, as all dragon-keepers live within the dragon colony itself. He would, however, be allowed to visit home from time to time and he could certainly communicate with his family using the usual postal system. Eli would be expected to begin his training with the most menial tasks within the dragon colony; with no complaints allowed. He would report to his dragon supervisor and ultimately to the Dragon King himself. If the Dragon King was at any time dissatisfied with his performance, Eli could be released from his position, or in severe circumstances, destroyed.

"Do you understand these conditions, Eli, or would you like some time to consider whether or not you will accept the position of dragon-keeper?" Oliver looked squarely at Eli with this final question.

"Yes, sir, I understand everything you have explained, and no, I do not need more time to think about this. I have always wished to become a dragon-keeper and nothing you say is going to stop me!"

The crowd let out a deafening cheer as Eli smiled down at them. Even Master Oliver applauded Eli.

From that moment on Eli's life would never be the same.

After the official ceremony was completed and the crowd began to disperse, Mother handed Eli a duffle containing his favorite clothes and a few of his personal belongings. Eli hugged her goodbye in haste and followed the council leaders who waited to escort him to the dragon colony. There he was introduced to members of the dragon colony, its council of elder dragons, and even the glorious Dragon King, Zonar, who also congratulated him on being chosen, much to Eli's surprise. Then Zonar astounded Eli by telling him the dragons had been watching him for years.

"Watching me? How? I've never even met a dragon until today. I've only seen you flying over town."

"True, but we know a great deal about you, Eli," Zonar answered with kindness. "Now I would like to introduce you to your direct supervisor, Zelina."

Chapter 2

Kane

Jolara. To the far north of Zimley and across the western sea, hidden from view by dense forests, lay the land of Jolara. Her people, the Jolarans, had nothing to do with anyone or anything outside their forested world. A visitor here would note the stark differences between Jolara and Zimley, though there were never visitors to Jolara. Where the people of Zimley worked at a variety of business ventures, manufacturing, trade, and agriculture, the people of Jolara lived quite simply and completely off the land. There were no businesses; no need for education or trade. Each Jolaran family built their own home, more of a hut really, and worked together to harvest food from the forest. That meant gathering ripe fruits, gleaning edible leaves and hunting wildlife.   There were often battles between Jolaran families, some wanting to take over the best hunting and foraging lands and protect them for their own use. Most often, the stronger family dominated the area and drove the weaker families out, leaving them to migrate deeper into the forest or risk following the dangerous and forbidden coastline to new hunting grounds.

Such was the life of young Kane, the son of a once-strong Jolaran family. But since his father's death during a battle for hunting grounds, Kane's family was no longer considered powerful. Kane, his mother, Anaya, and younger brother, Devon, had been displaced five times in the last year. Each time the task had fallen to Kane to move his family to the safety and hopeful security of new hunting and foraging areas where they would not be threatened. At least for a while.

On this particular morning, nothing seemed unusual as Kane rose with the first light of dawn. He rubbed the sleep from his dark brown eyes, and slipped his soft deerskin tunic over his head, not noticing the tousled state of his thick, dark brown hair. Kane breathed in deeply, noticing again how the air smelled of smoke, much stronger than the smoke from a small cooking fire. He scanned the sky but saw no signs of forest fire. Kane rekindled the family's small fire in preparation for his mother, picked up a spear and strode into the dense forest surrounding the family hut. Tall, strong, and with a wiry athletic build, Kane moved on silent feet. He watched and listened, pausing between nearly every step. Kane knew well the sounds of forest animals: night dwellers returning to their burrows for a good day's rest and the day folk of the forest just beginning to stir. There was a distant rumbling sound off in the distance. Kane froze, listening intently. Then, movement in the underbrush to his right claimed his attention away. A quick and accurate thrust of his spear and Kane had a plump squirrel for breakfast. One more and he would head back to the fire.

When he returned to the hut, Anaya was heating water over the fire, while Devon was busy cracking nuts the boys had gathered only the day before. Kane held out his catch to Mother.

"What a fine provider you are for us, son,"

"Thank you, Mother, but it's not much," Kane always felt embarrassment when she praised him for doing what was just his responsibility.

With that the small family settled around the fire to enjoy their morning meal together. Anaya thanked the Creator for their provisions and asked Him to guide family in light and truth. Afterward Kane and Devon moved across the clearing to sharpen new spears and arrows from long branches Kane had brought back from the forest, each one strong and sturdy.

Kane heard them coming: Nantell and his five burly sons, stomping through the forest underbrush, breaking tender shoots and frightening small game. Nantell's family had driven them farther south only a few weeks earlier. Kane had barely had time to build a new shelter amidst all the hunting he and Devon had to do in this new area. Now they were back. He ran to warn his mother.

"No, Kane, not this time. We can't fight Nantell again. We both know we will just lose." His mother spoke with a resigned firmness in her voice that was foreign to her usual gentle way. "No, this time we give them what they want and leave."

"Mother, I can't believe you are even suggesting that!" Kane was outraged. "Nantell thinks he can take over leadership of our clan if he keeps driving us out. Everyone knows that only the weakest families move without defending their hunting grounds!"

"I know what everyone thinks. But sometimes it takes courage to do what is right in the face of what others think. You and I both know that Devon has still not recovered from the last battle with Nantell's sons. I don't want to lose him like we did your father. Or you either, for that matter.

"Kane, we both know Nantell is nothing like your father. He will rule our clan with brute force and fear. I know that leadership should have fallen to you and you would lead with the same gentleness and mercy that your father did, just as the Creator calls us to do. But Kane, you know the truth. You must protect your brother and the only way to do that is to get far away from Nantell."

Kane looked over at Devon, wispy brown hair falling in waves around his innocent face and a questioning look in his eager hazel eyes. He still limped from wounds inflicted in their last battle with Nantell's family. So young, only eight and he had endured so much. Through his anger and dismay, Kane realized that Mother was right. They must go, and far.

"Devon, you help Mother gather our supplies and hunting weapons. We're leaving," Kane announced with authority just as Nantell broke into the clearing. Kane picked up his bow and rose to meet the tall hunter. As Kane faced the clan he lowered his bow, a sign of defeat.

Nantell roared with laughter. "So, you admit defeat without a fight this time! Get off my land, you spineless scum."

Kane seethed inside, but held his tongue. "We'll be gone before nightfall. The clearing is yours, O Great and Powerful Nantell. All I ask is a few hours of daylight to gather our supplies and move on peacefully."

The oldest son snorted and laughed but Nantell waved him aside. "You have until sunset, or I do away with you, boy." Kane nodded his understanding as Nantell's youngest son, seven-year-old Maxell, raised his fist in victory.

~ ~ ~

And so began the most perilous journey of Kane's life. He felt the weight of responsibility heavy upon his shoulders. He had to protect his mother and brother, find a safe place in the forest and provide for their needs. Quite a heavy load for any fourteen-year-old son to carry, but carry it he did.

After they left the clearing and Nantell's clan behind, Kane heard sounds, unusual sounds in the distance behind them. Was that Nantell's son screaming? It was certainly not a victory yell. Kane found a secluded and densely covered pocket among the trees where he hid his family, then taking care not to make a single sound, he crept back toward the clearing, their former home. Brown eyes peering from beneath heavy branches, Kane saw an enormous creature standing over Nantell holding one of his sons aloft, its huge cat-like paw waving the young man as if he were a mere leaf. The creature was covered in thick blue fur, with a full greenish-black mane that cascaded around its muscular neck and down over protruding shoulders. It had the build of a mountain cat, only vastly larger. Its legs sported muscles that were strong and supple. Along the creature's back, sharply pointed green spikes sparkled in the sunlight. And on its head, the beast carried a pair of equally shinny horns that curved back on themselves. Nantell's son, Jared, was lifted overhead in one huge paw. Kane watched in terrified wonder as a tiny streamer-dart, the protective little birds of the forest, swatted its poison-tipped tail feathers into that huge blue paw. In most animals, the streamer-dart's poison caused immediate paralysis of the muscles, but not this creature. It batted at the tiny bird, took Jared in its jaws and shook him hard before tossing the youth to the rocks below. Jared's body landed with a sickening thud. The creature bent, with fangs as long as a man's hand, to take an enormous bite out of the now deceased young hunter. Nantell lunged at the creature, only to be knocked aside as one would down a small rodent. Kane noticed the paw had the longest, sharpest claws he had ever seen on

any forest animal. The creature roared in cruel delight and lumbered toward Tallon, Nantell's second born son, muscular shoulders rippling with every step.

Unsure of the origins of this ravenous monster, Kane was certain that the creature wanted the young, strong Jolarans. It was feeding time! He waited no longer, fearing he might be discovered. Kane moved with extra caution, loathe to give away his position to the strange and horrendous creature. Returning to his mother and Devon, Kane whispered the need for silence. He urged his family onward, away from the strange scene back at the clearing. Taking care to stay within the heaviest undergrowth, Kane steered his family farther south and to the east this time, carefully and surreptitiously heading toward the forbidden coastline. Forbidden for generations. Forbidden to ensure the preservation of the Jolaran people from certain doom.

Mary Harrison

Chapter 3

Apprentice in Training

Eli liked Zelina, his dragon supervisor, from the beginning. Zelina was among the oldest of the dragons, wrinkles and creases around her laughing eyes gave away her gleeful spirit. Zelina's rosy scales shimmered in the sunlight, enhancing her joyous countenance. She was kind and gentle with Eli, but also fun-loving and could make him laugh, especially at himself when he had difficulty learning his tasks. And there were many tasks to learn. Eli started out slowly and easily enough, learning to maintain each dragon's personal living cave and the nuances desired by each dragon occupant. Before long he moved on to dragon grooming, a rather difficult task at best. Each dragon required its scales to be polished regularly until they had an iridescent shine. Though they all looked intimidating at first, everyone in the dragon colony seemed to appreciate the grooming and all were gentle and kind to Eli. Soon, this task was not such a problem for Eli with the smaller dragons. It was only the oldest and largest of the dragons that caused Eli to fear. He was not entirely sure why, for all his life Eli had heard stories of the gentle dragons of Zimzor. Now, however, as a young apprentice looking into the eyes of these formidable beasts, Eli was not so sure all of those old stories were anything but legends.

The day eventually came when Eli was assigned to groom Zonar. With trembling hands he began polishing the scales on Zonar's massive chest. Just as Eli had begun to feel slightly less small and intimidated, Zonar curved his serpentine neck down where his immense head could look Eli directly in the eyes.

"You have nothing to fear from me, young Eli. Remember, you are here at my request. I have seen and observed your development for many years now. I understand what is in your heart, your great desire to please, care and love. You are exactly the kind of new dragon-keeper we wanted."

"Y-y-yes, sir," Eli stuttered.

"But you still fear me?"

Eli stopped his polishing process. "I'm afraid so, Zonar. There is just something in the eyes of dragons, especially the oldest and largest ones that does not seem all that safe. Perhaps your eyes look a little …well…wild to me."

Zonar tipped back his head and let out a roaring laugh. His eyes danced as his gaze met Eli's again. "Yes, Eli, you are the most perceptive new dragon-keeper we have had for a great, long time now. You are correct. We dragons are always wild and free creatures, never to be owned or controlled by others, just as the Creator meant it to be. But, I assure you that you have nothing to fear from any of us. You are totally safe and protected here within the caves of the dragon colony. No harm can ever come to you. Now, my scales, if you please."

With that Eli felt strangely calmed and returned to his grooming. As he worked and his mind steadied, he was able to concentrate on the incredible colors of each scale that he polished. No two were exactly alike, just as no two dragons ever appeared alike in color. Zonar's scales radiated a vast array of blues, greens, pinks and lavenders. *He really is striking and beautiful,* Eli marveled at the artistic creativity evident in each dragon scale. If there ever was a part of creation that could convince a person of the guiding hand of the creator, dragon scales would have to be Eli's first choice for evidence.   He stood back admiring Zonar's scales as light danced and shimmered in waves across his body, awaiting Zonar's approval.

Chapter 4

Finding Refuge

They traveled for six days, stopping only for minimal rest. Kane refused to allow an evening fire for cooking or warmth. He insisted his family sleep under cover of the most sheltered tree branches and only gather what food they could find as they traveled. There was no time for a hunting foray. Devon limped to keep up with Kane's pace, never complaining, though exhaustion showed on his face. Anaya kept a concerned watch over Devon, so small and thin for his age, as Kane insisted they push onward in silence.

No one was sure who the first to notice was, but the early afternoon air took on a new and refreshing smell. Soon the small band of travelers became aware of a different sound underlying the familiar sounds of the forest; a soft, dull roar. Kane realized that they were nearing his goal. He turned his family a bit more to the east. Following the sound, he wove them through the trees and down a steep slope. And all of a sudden, as the family broke through the trees, there it was! The coast: forbidden, yet possessing a beauty and power like nothing found within the forest. Kane stood in awe as he watched the waves crashing on the rocks below.

"I cannot believe you have done this to our family! Kane, how could you? How could you lead us to the forbidden land of the coast?" Anaya cried.

"Mother, I told you there is great danger behind us and it is no longer from Nantell and his family. This new danger is much more fearsome. Somehow, deep inside, I felt this was the only safe place for us," Kane responded to his frantic mother with a gentle voice, trying to sound calmer than he felt. "I will tell you the truth of everything I saw back at our clearing, but first we must find shelter for the night. Do you know if the tales of caves along the coast are true?"

Anaya breathed deeply, trying to regain some sense of calm before she responded. "I don't know, son, I never thought about whether the tales are true or not. They have been told and retold for as long as anyone can remember. Why, I can still remember your grandfather taking me as a little girl on his knee by the evening fire," Anaya's eyes were wistful as she recounted her memories. "His eyes would twinkle in the firelight as he embellished the old dragon tales, trying to scare me. Oh, how he loved it when I would tremble and squeal. But are they real? I have no idea – the tales just are."

"I don't remember the tales much. No one tells the tales since Father died." Devon's intense loss was evident in the frustration carried in his voice as he spoke.

"Then I'll tell you one of the tales, Devon. Tonight," Kane replied, "after we find shelter."

There was a brief debate about leaving Anaya with the supplies and the boys searching the coast for a cave. The debate ended almost before it began, as Anaya would not hear of her precious, though very brave, sons exploring the forbidden and surely dangerous coast alone. And so, the little band started down the slope, climbing over rocky crags, moving ever nearer to the beach below.

"Look!" Devon cried, pointing to his right.

Sure enough, not far from their present position along the cliff, there seemed to be an opening, only a short distance above the beach. A cave!

"Well done, Devon. You have found our shelter for tonight," Kane congratulated his brother. "I see that you will grow to be a fine provider yourself someday." Kane repeated the words of encouragement he had often heard from his father when he was younger, still learning the ways of his people. Kane's heart swelled as he watched Devon's face glow with happiness and pride at such a wonderful accomplishment. Together the boys helped and encouraged their mother across huge boulders, making their way along the cliff face toward the cave.

A short time later, they had gathered enough wood from the beach for a fire in the mouth of the cave. A warm and wonderful fire. Leaving Anaya to unpack the supplies and set up camp within the cave, Kane took Devon and the spears down to the water's edge and slowly waded in. Before long he had speared several small fish for dinner. Even Devon succeeded in making a catch, another opportunity for Kane to praise his younger brother for his honorable skills.

With the fish cooked and their aching stomachs truly full for the first time in days, the small family settled down among their furs, cozy behind the fire and feeling safe at last. Devon looked up with hopeful eyes.

"Kane, remember the legends? You promised," he began.

"Yes, Devon, I sure did. Are you ready to hear of the greatest battle of all time?"

Devon nodded and snuggled against his mother.

Mary Harrison

Chapter 5

The Dragon Nursery

Eli's training continued and before long he found himself reassigned to the dragon nursery, a most respected position for any apprentice keeper. Eli enjoyed the daily routine of cleaning, warming and rotating each dragon egg. Each nest required careful tending. Temperatures had to be maintained within strict limits if the young lives inside were to develop fully.

Today had been a day Eli was certain he would never forget, for the day had finally come

when he witnessed his first dragon hatching. He was rotating the sparkling blue egg when it began trembling in his hands. This particular egg was one of the largest eggs Eli had cared for so far. It was, in fact, so large that to pick it up was an armload for Eli. Wide-eyed, Eli knelt beside the nest and

watched as the trembling became a rhythmic rocking. Before long, the egg split neatly in two. The most beautiful young dragon uncurled itself, looked up at Eli and toppled over on unsteady legs.

Eli had been trained in what actions should come next. He quickly scooped up the little dragon and carried it over to the warming nests. Here a hatchling would be kept warm until it could regulate its own body temperature outside the egg; usually only a few days were required. Next Eli brought food to his little charge. Baby dragons required a mostly meat diet, like all dragons, except they are unable to chew many of the tougher meats preferred by older dragons. Instead, the dragon nursery kept a supply of tender cuts of meat, boiled, shredded and mashed, ready for the hatchlings. Eli marveled at the beauty of this new dragon as he patiently fed small mouthfuls of the mash to him. His scales were a chocolate brown, but Eli could tell they would soon radiate pinks, yellows and lavenders, a most unusual combination for any dragon's colors. After the baby dragon was settled and resting in the nest, Eli went to report the birth to Zelina.

Throughout the morning Eli continued his tasks in the nursery. Before stopping for his own lunch Eli found a most surprising honor bestowed upon him. Two of the dragon elders, Zonar and Dentax, came to visit the nursery and inspect the new hatchling. Eli presumed they wanted to check on its progress. Dentax called Eli over to the warming nest.

"What shall you call him?" Dentax asked, looking squarely at Eli.

"Me? You want me to name him?" Eli could not believe his ears!

"Do not be dismayed, Eli," Zonar now spoke. "It is a great honor for a dragon-keeper to be allowed to name a hatchling. We now give you that honor." He almost appeared to bow his head towards Eli.

In amazement, Eli reached over to the hatchling and studied his eyes, scales; every part of him right down to the tip of his little tail. "Roan," he said at last. "I'd like to call him Roan... if you please, sirs."

"Then Roan it shall be," declared Dentax with a gleam in his eyes.

For the rest of the day Eli worked in a daze. After he had checked on all the eggs in his section of the nursery, he went back to Roan. Eli spent more than a few minutes watching his regular breathing, studying every detail of his little body. Eli knew how fast dragons grew. It would be no time at all before Roan was larger that Eli, even though Eli himself had grown quite a bit in the last few months.

As this amazing day gave way to twilight, Eli stood at the cave entrance watching brilliant colors being painted across the evening sky of Zimzor. It was always a dazzling show as the twin suns slowly sunk to the southwest of the caves. First the larger sun painted gleaming streaks across the sky as it moved toward the horizon, only to be followed by even more spectacular colors as the smaller, yet brighter, of the binary pair took its turn creating an almost magical sky. Since his earliest memories, this was Eli's favorite time of day. His young dragon charge was safely tucked away for the night and Eli had a little time to himself before he, too, turned in. As darkness enveloped the caves, Eli turned to go inside. Tyffan, another apprentice two years older than Eli, waited just inside the cave.

"Congratulations, Eli. I've never seen another apprentice allowed to name a dragon before. We're all very proud of you." She spoke with a soft shyness.

"Thanks. I don't know why Zonar would pick me for such an honor."

"Because everyone can see how special you are. Everyone except you, that is." Tyffan stifled a gentle laugh. "Well, good night, Eli."

"Good night." Eli thought about Tyffan's words. Was she speaking the truth or just teasing him? He was unsure, yet he felt a deep satisfaction inside. He loved his work and was proud to call the dragon caves home. With that Eli settled down to sleep.

Chapter 6

Father's Legend

"A long time ago, the lands of Jolara extended far and wide, beyond the vast forests and across the Great Sea. Our ancestors built rafts, canoes and even larger boats to sail across the sea. The brave explorers found a rich and beautiful land on the far side of the sea."

Kane closed his eyes as he tried to remember every detail of the legend his father told him so many times as a young child. When he opened them again, his eyes met Devon's intent gaze.

"The travelers found forests and meadows rich with life; animals for hunting, plants loaded with fruits and vegetables ripe for the picking. They also found people, different from our own, yet the same as well. These new people called themselves the Zimleys. They became very angry when they saw our ancestors hunting in their forests and gathering the fruits and vegetables. They said the land with its plants and animals belonged to the Zimleys and they would not share its bounty with our travelers.

"Worse than that, the Zimleys laughed at our Jolaran ancestors, for they said our people were primitive. They claimed to have a better way of life, growing 'crops' to harvest and process for food, raising captive animals so no hunting was necessary.

"No one knows exactly what happened next. Our people say they only wanted to share the rich treasures of the land. Their people say that our ancestors stole from them. Either way, everyone forgot to seek wisdom, guidance and truth from the Creator and the dispute soon led to fighting. The Zimleys were weaker and inexperienced fighters, but there were many more of them. Even so, our hunters fought with great courage. For a time it looked as if the Jolarans would win even larger hunting grounds. But the Zimleys were very clever. They set traps and had unusual and powerful weapons. Many of our people died in the battle for food and hunting grounds across the sea. The battle raged on for a very long time. Our people sent our strongest and bravest fighters across the sea to do battle for the land. Their people devised new traps at every turn.

"Just when the Jolarans were about to defeat the Zimleys completely, something dreadful appeared. Down out of the sky swooped huge and frightening beasts, their wings a great expanse that seemed to fill the sky."

"Dragons," whispered Devon.

"Yes, dragons! The most fearsome beasts our people had ever seen at that time. Well, the dragons went to the aid of the Zimleys without a moment's hesitation. Our people were lifted into the sky and dashed on rocks below. Many more were killed in the powerful jaws of these awesome, winged warriors.

"In the end, those that remained alive were carried across the sea and deposited here on the Eastern coast. The most immense dragon of all instructed our once brave ancestors that they must live deep within the forests and never dwell on the coast again. Any who dared to cross the sea would immediately be put to death by the dragons.

"And just to make certain that our people obeyed his words, that great dragon lord ordered his beasts to continually patrol the coastline, searching for wayward Jolarans."

"And that is why we call it the *Forbidden Coast*?" asked Devon. "But is it true? Did the dragons really exist?"

"That, my brother is what we must find out tomorrow," Kane answered Devon while fixing his eyes on his mother. Hers was an expression mixed with fear and disbelief, yet also laced with a little pride for the bravery of her son.

Chapter 7

Another Family Honor

Eli rose early, allowing himself time for a refreshing morning run on the beach at sunrise before his duties in the nursery began. He had stopped by the nursery to make sure his little charges were all still resting before heading out to the beach.

Eli had been privileged to be present for the hatching of all seven eggs in the clutch he was assigned to tend. Each small dragon was a new experience in wonder, beauty and amazing color.

As these small reptilian creatures grew and began to learn about life, it was Eli who was there tending them, watching out for their well being, and teaching them everything a young dragon would need to know.

This morning all seven still slept soundly, so Eli felt confident that he had plenty of time to enjoy some exercise and quiet time on his own. He ran with an easy loping gait, splashing in the early morning waves as the twin suns began to streak glorious colors across the sky over the cliffs of the dragon colony. Lost in thought, Eli reflected on the many blessings in his life; his loving family who so willingly allowed him to take the job of his dreams even though it meant living away from home, his position as an apprentice dragon-keeper living among the amazing and kind dragons in their private colony, his friends here at the colony especially Tyffan and Zelina. *The Creator has given me incredible blessings in my short life. More than some people have in an entire lifetime.* Eli gave thanks for his wonderful life as he turned and ran back toward the entrance to the colony.

Breathing hard from his finishing sprint, Eli strode up the path heading toward his own dwelling cave, only to be met by Zonar at the main entrance to the colony.

"Good morning, sir," Eli gasped between deep breaths.

"Yes, it is Eli. Every day the Creator makes is a glorious one, don't you think? Did you enjoy your run today?" Zonar greeted Eli before sharing his news. "Today you will go into Zimley with me, Eli. Your presence is required at the town council meeting today."

"Me, at the council meeting? Whatever for, Zonar?"

"It seems you have another family member to be honored by the council today. Your father has been elected to the new arbiter seat on the council. His intellectual research and passion for fairness and mercy have won him this esteemed position. We feel that you should be present at his swearing in to honor and support your father in his new post."

Eli smiled. "You've just described my father so well. I'm happy and excited for him. What time is the ceremony?"

"Several of our dragon elders will also be attending. We shall leave within the hour, which should give you plenty of time to change and ask Tyffan or one of the other keepers to watch over your charges in the nursery while you are away." Turning to go back inside the caves, Zonar added,

"Tremor, Dentax, Rosamae and I shall meet you on the beach when you are ready to leave."

Eli hurried to bathe, and then found Tyffan, already about her tasks in the dragon nursery. She was tending a clutch of five eggs that were just beginning to hatch.

"Hey Tyffan, I need a favor."

"You do? What sort of favor, Eli?"

"Zonar just told me that my father is being sworn in as a new town council member today. He wants me to attend to show support for my dad and I wouldn't want to miss this for anything. Could you watch over my little ones for the morning?"

Tyffan smiled her sweet, shy smile. "Sure Eli, I can do that. But only if you tell me all about it when you get back."

"Deal! I have a few minutes left before I have to meet Zonar and the other elders on the beach to leave for town. I can help you get their morning meal ready."

A short time later, Eli was waiting on the beach feeling a growing sense of excitement in anticipation of his father's honor. Zonar and the other elders emerged from the colony entrance.

"Climb aboard, Eli," Zonar called as he strolled down the path. "No sense in you running all the way to town while we make the short flight."

Eli's eyes widened. "Excuse me, sir. You mean ride on your back?"

Dentax and the others laughed heartily at Eli's dismay.

"Certainly, Eli. In ages past, we dragons flew with riders on our backs quite regularly. But that's a long story." Zonar knelt down while Eli climbed up his foreleg and onto his shoulder. "Make yourself comfortable in front of my shoulder spine. Now, since I don't happen to have a saddle with me, you'll have to hold tightly to my neck."

A trembling Eli settled himself atop Zonar's massive shoulders and reached around Zonar's enormous neck, attempting a firm grip. Zonar and the other dragons spread their wings, jumped into the air and beat their massive wings toward the town of Zimley, a very astounded Eli along for an amazing ride.

Eli for his part marveled at the sights of the forest below him. He easily recognized the familiar path that he traveled between the dragon colony and the town on visits to his family. The town appeared tiny, like a toy village below him, as the dragons circled above. Gentle curving arcs above town and the dragons began their descent, each landing with smooth grace on the forest side of the massive governmental building.

At Zonar's biding, Eli released his death grip on Zonar's wide, scale-encrusted neck and slide down the giant reptile's foreleg, landing on shaking legs. With a gentle push from his massive head, Zonar directed a still stunned Eli around the governmental building to the town square where he could rendezvous with his family prior to the swearing in ceremony. Eli sat down on a bench in front of the building to collect his thoughts and wait for his family.

"Eli, what are you doing here?" Marina ran to greet her beloved and now famous older brother.

"Zonar told me about Dad's election to the council. I'm here for the swearing in ceremony. And what about you, little sister? Skipping school today, I see!"

Marina grinned; always glad to enjoy some lighthearted teasing from her brother. "Yes," she answered, "my friends in class need more information about the dragon colony direct from our favorite dragon-keeper."

"Hey you two, are you ready to go inside?" Dawson Harcourt strode up alongside the children with their mother, Clarice, at his side. Eli greeted his parents with hugs and congratulations as the family climbed the steps of the auspicious building together.

Inside as Master Oliver convened the council meeting with one of his long-winded speeches, Eli only half listened. Eyes perusing the council chambers, a room Eli had only been in once before, he noticed the floor to ceiling double windows across the far wall all standing open to the forest beyond. Zonar and the other dragons looked in on the council, one from each window. Zonar caught the surprised expression on Eli's face and winked at him from his vantage point outside. Just then, Oliver called Dawson Harcourt to stand before the council.

"As the newly elected arbiter for the Zimley town council, it will fall to you, Dawson Harcourt, to administer fair and sound judgment in cases of dispute that require the council's deliberation for the sake of the people of Zimley. Your vote will be cast as all other members of the council upon enactment of new laws. However, in cases where there may be a tie amongst the votes of council members, it will be your responsibility to research the potential outcomes of pending legislation before the council. You will then bring recommendations and options before the council prior to a revote. Do you understand these responsibilities as I have outlined them to you?"

"Yes, sir, I do."

"Then we shall proceed with the swearing in."

Eli watched, full of love and pride for his father, as Oliver administered the oath of office.

"Do you, Dawson Harcourt, solemnly swear to uphold the laws of Zimley, act with sound and wise judgment, and seek the wisdom of our Creator prior to making any judgments for the people or recommendations to the council?"

Dawson stood erect, focused on every word of the oath he was about to take. "I do," he responded.

"Then, with the power vested in me by the people of Zimley as mayor of this town, I pronounce you our newest council member, with all the responsibilities and privileges therein." Oliver shook Dawson's hand vigorously to the applause of other council members, as well as Clarice, Eli and Marina.

From the window Zonar cleared his throat after allowing for a reasonable time of applause and congratulations around the room. Oliver visibly stiffened at the interruption, but the colossal dragon only raised one eyebrow and pretended not to notice. "Mr. Harcourt, on behalf of the dragon elders, I want to express my congratulations to you as well. We look forward to working with you on all matters concerning the protection of Zimley and the well being of the dragon colony. I have no doubt that we at the dragon colony will be as pleased with your work as we are with Eli's performance."

Dawson bowed graciously toward the massive dragon king. "Lord Zonar, thank you. I, too, look forward to working with the dragons as well as the town council. I only hope that I can measure up to your expectations half as well as my son." Dragons and council members alike laughed and jovial conversation flowed between the council and dragons for the next while.

"Eli, can you join us for an early luncheon before returning to the dragon colony?" Clarice asked her son as things began to wind down in the council chambers.

"I don't know, Mom. I have seven young dragons to tend to in the nursery."

Zonar interjected before Eli could turn down the opportunity for lunch with his family. "Eli, I believe your young charges are in good hands. Why between Zelina and Tyffan, they will be not only well cared for, but most probably, spoiled little dragons by the time you return. I think you have plenty of time to enjoy lunch with your family," eyes twinkling, Zonar turned his focus toward

Marina as he continued, "Just as long as you escort your sister back to school before you return. I wouldn't want one of my keepers to have a little sister who made a habit of truancy."

"No problem! Thanks, Zonar," Eli nudged Marina, who giggled as the family turned to leave.

Chapter 8

Midnight Conference

It had been several hours since Kane told Father's legend. Devon slept soundly covered by furs. Anaya's breathing was soft and rhythmic. Darkness enveloped the cave. Kane lay still and listened to the night sounds of the coast. The roar of the waves and the splash of the sea covered most other sounds. He could barely make out the caw of a sea bird in the distance, but he heard none of the familiar sounds of the forest. No rustling leaves as small night animals made their way in search of food. No owls hooting in the distance. This coastline was a strange and mysterious land.

Unable to sleep, Kane silently made his way to the mouth of the cave. He sat and stirred the embers of the fire, rekindling a small flame. As he contemplated their situation, he was surprised by a gentle hand on his shoulder. Without a sound, Anaya sat down beside him, her deep brown hair cascading down over her fine shoulders.

"Kane, my brave son, you must tell me what happened back at our clearing."

Kane looked deep into his mother's face in the dim firelight. Zimzor's three moons cast a blue halo about her wavy hair, bestowing an ethereal glow about her. Kane hardly knew how to begin.

"Mother, do you remember Father's other favorite legend – the one about the tarkoza that live hidden in the slopes of the smoking mountains?"

"Of course I remember. That was always his favorite way to make you squeal and tremble."

"Do you think either of the legends is true?"

Anaya was thoughtful and quiet for several minutes before answering. "Hmmm…My grandfather seemed to believe in the dragon legend, at least enough to instill a great fear of the coast in all of us," she recalled. "But as for the tarkoza, I don't think anyone ever thought that was anything

more than just a child's fantasy." She gazed intently into his face, "Why, Kane, what did you see?"

"When I heard Jared screaming, it was not like any victory scream, or even any scream of pain that I could ever remember. So I had to know what was happening. When I returned to our clearing, I peered through the lower branches of my hiding place and what I saw turned my stomach in knots.

"There was a huge creature, more than twice a man's height when it stood on all four paws. When it reared up on its hind legs it must have been at least as tall as three men, maybe four. It was strong and muscular, with thick shaggy blue fur. Its teeth were long and curved, more so than any meat-eater we have ever hunted. It had Jared, first in its paws, then in its jaws. It reared up on hind legs and shook him like an old worn out fur. Its paws were huge, bigger than paws on any animal I have ever seen. And with those paws, it knocked Nantell aside as easily as if he were a child's toy.

"Mother, it has to be the tarkoza." Kane paused to think and let this information sink in.

"I remember my grandfather told me the tarkoza only come out when the mountains smoke," Anaya recalled.

"Do you remember the rumbling sounds and burning smells in the air lately," Kane asked. "Do you think the mountains have awakened these beasts?"

"It would seem so. Then if the beasts of the legend actually do exist, and I have no doubt that is what you have seen, my son, then what they do to our people is also true." Anaya's voice was filled with fear and recollection as she pondered the old legend. She realized the truth that the beasts from the legend had, in, fact just awakened.

"Father used to say the tarkoza ate our people until only a few survived. Then when the mountains quit smoking, they returned to their hidden caves to hibernate once again. They're going to eat us all."

"Not all," Anaya said quietly, "Legend has it that they always feast on the young strong hunters first. Then as they have their fill, the beasts are said to move on to other members of the clans, older and weaker ones are not as desirable for a meal it seems. According to my grandfather, some of our people always manage to survive. He must be right, Kane. After all, we're here, aren't we?" Some of the old gleam was returning to her eyes.

Silence filled the space between them as mother and son each contemplated their situation given this new information.

"You have a plan, don't you my son?"

"I wouldn't exactly call it much of a plan, but I do have an idea," Kane began to explain. "When I saw what those creatures were doing to Nantell's family, I felt the coast was the only reasonably safe place for us. The caves will offer us some shelter and protection for the time being." Kane paused, trying to find courage before he continued.

"I know it is forbidden and I even understand why. But the legends say these beasts can remain awakened for many months. If we are to survive this period of attack from these creatures, we need help."

Anaya's eyes suddenly widened with understanding. "No, Kane, you can't do it," she croaked forcefully.

"Mother, the tarkoza are real – and very hungry. Our only hope is in finding the dragons, assuming those are also real. I think you believe that, too. If we don't, then we are nothing more than prisoners in this cave, waiting for the tarkoza to find us, too.

"You've always taught me the words of our Creator; that anyone who seeks the truth will find it, and that truth will set us free. Mother, I believe that the legends have been our people's way of remembering the truths from the Creator, passed down from our ancestors. Now one of those legends has come back to life; vicious, hungry and with a look of evil that I've never seen in any animal's eyes before. We need someone or something to save us. And I am placing my hope in the legend of the dragons. They came to save the people from across the sea, perhaps we can convince them to save our people now. Devon and I must begin looking for clues in the morning." Kane ended with such final authority in his voice that his mother could only nod in agreement.

Mary Harrison

Chapter 9

Training

Eli was allowed to raise and work with young Roan and the months together passed quickly. His budding dragon charge had grown with surprising speed. It had only been a matter of a few weeks before Roan's height matched Eli's. Now after four months, Roan towered over Eli, as all the dragons did. His eyes were friendly and full of life. A fun-loving life. Roan enjoyed nothing more than a good game of tag with other young dragons or perhaps a game of flying catch with Eli.

Although it did not seem so to the half-grown dragons, each of the "games" the keepers played with them served a purpose. Some built flying strength, others maneuvering skill, still others developed a keen sense of observation. And through all of the games, Roan always looked to Eli, for it was Eli who was always there to encourage him. It didn't matter whether Roan missed an important catch, landed with less grace than expected or misjudged his distance and crashed into a tree rather than skimming over it. Eli would understand. He always understood Roan, and always forgave his mistakes and praised his successes.

For Eli these days of training had been a natural transition from his duties in the dragon nursery. He relished following the growth and participating in the training of the clutch of seven dragons he had hatched and cared for. Seven youthful dragons was quite a large responsibility for an apprentice dragon-keeper, but Eli handled his duties with natural ease. Despite his love for all of his reptilian flock, Roan was his favorite.

Today the dawn had been particularly beautiful with the twin suns rising over the caves in a spectacular display of colorful hues. Eli had his dragon charges out on the beach early for a morning coastal flight. These supervised flights helped prepare fledgling dragons for the extended flights and patrols across the sea, along Jolara's forbidden coast.

Zelina kept a watchful eye on Eli's progress training the growing dragons. Only the evening before she had encouraged Eli to push Roan, extend his endurance and introduce him to flights over the water. She smiled and nodded as Eli began his morning workout with his training group. He always took her so seriously and Zelina was pleased with everything she witnessed on this beautiful morning.

Eli began with a gentle flight so the dragons could enjoy the morning breezes. Then he challenged a race from the cave entrance to the forest line just before the town of Zimley. He watched and cheered as Roan and Celeste, a beautiful female dragon with scales in the loveliest hues of reds, pinks and yellows, quickly moved out in front of the others. This striking pair battled each other for lead position. Then, as naturally as if he had planned it, both dragons arced out over the water, soaring in a graceful semicircle for their race back to the caves. Neither of the juvenile dragons seemed to notice the time over the water, as they were too intent on their quest to finish first. When

they descended to land, Roan touched down first,
tripped and rolled in a somersault. Celeste glided
gracefully down beside him, peals of laughter
ringing from both dragons. Eli jogged up the beach
cheering and congratulating all the dragons.

"That was great! Roan and Celeste, I'm so proud of you! You both went so far out over the water and your flight was strong and beautiful," Eli turned to the other dragons, "And look at you! You all followed them over the water! Wonderful! You are the best group of all the dragons in training!"

Just then, Eli and his dragon friends noticed Tyffan and her five dragon charges, all only three months old and not yet training with such intensity. The small group had witnessed the race from the cave entrance and was now cheering and flapping wings in approval. Tyffan strolled down the path to Eli.

"Nice work Eli. I've never seen a group of fledgling dragons take out over the water with such ease before. I spent three weeks encouraging my first group to do what you just accomplished. I don't know why, but some of the little ones often seem to be afraid of flying over the water."

"Thanks, Tyffan, but I don't think I did anything all that unusual. I just made a game out of it and they did the rest. This is just a very special group of burgeoning dragons."

"You're right, Eli. Everyone can see that. I'm sure that's why Zelina put you in charge of them. They are the best fliers and the most intelligent I've ever seen."

Eli felt himself blush at her praise. In his time at the dragon colony, Eli had formed many friendships, but none as special as Tyffan. He had found a kindred spirit in Tyffan. One wholly devoted to her work, intensely dedicated in all she did with a deep love for the dragons. Tyffan worked with a gentle kindness toward the dragons and her fellow keepers. She was Eli's best barometer to his own performance. It was Tyffan who most willingly gave out praise or tactfully offered pointers for improvement. Eli never took offense when Tyffan corrected him and always considered her compliments as the most genuine. Eli had his days when he wondered what he would do without her at the colony.

"Well, they are becoming very capable fliers, but they're also going to be hungry after that race. I'd better take care of that right now," Eli responded with a smile.

Chapter 10

The Search Begins

The morning dawned clear and brilliant as the twin suns rose from the east over the sea. Devon and Kane watched the display of colors from the cave entrance. After a brief meal of leftover fish, the pair set off to explore the beach.

"Today we search for dragons," Kane exclaimed bravely to his brother.

Devon's eyes widened in disbelief. "Where will we find them?"

"I don't know, but just keep looking up real

often," declared Kane as he splashed Devon and ran down the beach.

Together, Kane and Devon wandered farther south along the coast, noticing small crabs and shellfish in pools near water's edge. Kane thought there must be some edible meat on these unusual creatures and determined to take a few back to the cave. If anyone could figure out a way to cook them, he knew their mother could.

Before long, the boys discovered a thicket of ripe berries growing near the slopes of the cliffs and set about picking the sweet, delicious fruit. A real treasure to present to Mother! Kane ran back down the beach to collect a few large clam shells he had seen. These would make excellent bowls to carry the berries.

It was then, as he washed the sand off the shells in the gentle surf that it happened. Looking down to rinse the shells, a sudden darkness crossed over him. Eyes following the immense shadow on the sand, Kane's heart skipped a beat and his throat grew tight. He willed his eyes skyward and nearly fell over in the water at the sight he beheld. There it was above him, soaring over the cliffs. A dragon!

Huge.
Powerful.
Beautiful.

Frightening.

Devon! Kane's mind kicked into high gear and he tore back to his brother, tackling him into a heap under the berry bushes. Kane clamped his hand over Devon's mouth and whispered for silence. Devon struggled to nod his understanding. Not wanting to cause any noticeable movement, Kane carefully pointed a finger to the sky and turned his gaze northward. Peaking out from under Kane's protective arm, Devon began to tremble as his eyes froze on the terrible winged beast that patrolled the coast.

The boys watched, somewhat in awe and somewhat in fear, as far up the beach the great

dragon tipped its wings and made a graceful arc over the sea for a return flight south over their beach. Kane and Devon crouched lower under the berry thicket, each holding his breath. After what seemed like an eternity, the dragon turned and flapped its powerful wings eastward, back over the sea in the direction from which it had come.

Letting out a long sigh of relief, Kane and Devon sat up, still in shocked amazement after witnessing their first dragon. When it was long gone from sight, Kane declared it safe to move again. Warily, he crept back down to the water, retrieved his shells and returned to Devon and the berries. They wasted no time in filling their shell bowls. Kane kept them as close to the cliff rocks as possible while they returned to the cave. He wanted shelter available if need be. His eyes constantly scanned the sky for the dragon's return. None came.

Anaya listened intently as Devon recounted the tale for her. Eyes wistfully searching the sky, she longed to see the legendary creatures herself. They were true. All the old legends – and the beasts they told of were also true. Anaya was overcome with emotion; excitement, fear, trepidation, and wonder.

Kane broke into her thoughts. They would

need more food, so he and Devon were going back down to the beach to fish. After much debate, Kane convinced her that is was safe enough for them to catch some more fish, since the berries were not exactly a full meal. Kane reasoned that the dragon would not return for a while at least.

Anaya stood at the cave entrance, dividing her watchful gaze between her brave sons fishing in the surf, and the sky. Hoping at once to see a dragon and yet to not see one while the boys were so exposed. With enough fish in hand for the day, Kane and Devon returned to the cave to discuss what to do next.

Mary Harrison

Chapter 11

A Surprise Visit

After mealtime, with the dragons sunning themselves on the rocks above the shore, Eli headed down to the beach, kicked off his shoes and waded in. He let the waves lap at his feet and ankles as he enjoyed the suns' warm rays on his shoulders. The sea often mesmerized him and today was no different. Eli was lost in thoughts and the rhythm of the waves when a faint sound drifted into his consciousness. It sounded like someone calling. He focused on the sounds. A voice drifted from far down the beach. The voice was calling a name, but too distant to make out. Eli strained his eyes and saw a tiny figure way down the beach, just at the forest's edge.

That's odd. No one ever comes down the beach from the forest.

Thick forest separated the dragon colony from the Zimley's town and surrounding fields. The forest grew down to the cliffs and there was only treacherous, rocky coastline at that point, preventing any adventurous travelers from walking past the public beaches all the way to the dragon colony.

As Eli watched, the tiny figure grew into the form of a young girl, waving and calling. Then, Eli's eyes widened with recognition. Marina! Why would his sister be running down the beach toward him? He could hear her calling *his* name. What could she possibly be thinking? All the Zimleys knew that the only humans allowed into the dragon colony were the select few dragon keepers. There must be something tragically wrong for Marina to break such a steadfast town regulation.

Eli's heart pounded and he ran toward her through the water. As they approached each other, Eli noticed Marina's face for the first time. She did not show any indication of a mishap or crisis. Quite the opposite. Marina's face glowed. Her ecstatic grin stretched from ear to ear and her cheeks were rosy from the run.

"Eli, that was fantastic," Marina shouted and threw her arms around Eli, almost knocking him down. "I saw the race. Your dragons - they're so beautiful! Roan's getting so big!"

"You saw the race? How?"

Marina's excitement suddenly deflated; her secret out in the open.

"Marina, what have you been doing?" Eli questioned with a tone of accusation.

"I watch the dragons, sometimes." Her quiet reply had a note of shyness unusual for Marina.

"I don't understand. How? Where?"

"After school at the end of every week, I go for a walk to the beach, then down to the forest edge. I climb the rocks and sit on the highest peak so I can watch the dragons. Today we had a school holiday so I came early to watch, and I'm so glad I got to see the race. "

"Marina, that's so high. It's dangerous. And forbidden. No one is supposed to watch the dragons except the keepers."

"I know, but they're so wonderful I just can't help it. Besides, Zonar told me it was alright."

"Zonar? You've talked with Zonar, the

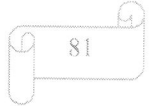

dragon king?" Eli could not believe what he was hearing.

"Sure, but I didn't know he was their king." Marina responded with reverence in her voice at this awe inspiring revelation. "He comes to visit with me on the rocks. The first time I met him I was climbing up to the peak when I slipped and fell. Zonar swooped from the sky and caught me. He landed with me on the rocks. I had to tell him the truth that I'd been watching dragons for a quite while."

Eli gulped. "What did he do to you?"

"Do to me?" Marina's expression was puzzled. "Nothing. He just tipped his head back and laughed. He told me they hadn't had a devoted dragon watcher for a long time. Then Zonar told me not to bring anyone else when I come to watch. I told Mother and Father, but I've never brought them with me. Ever since then, I always watch for Zonar to be out flying. Sometimes he comes down to meet me and we just sit and talk."

Now it was Eli's turn to be puzzled. He never knew that others had watched the dragons from the rocky cliffs. As Eli gave this idea some thought, he wondered if this might be how the Zimleys first came to know the dragons, through a few adventurous souls daring to climb the cliffs and watch the unknown. His thoughts were broken by Marina's next question.

"How did you get Roan to fly over the water so easily?"

"I made a game of it and he flew out over the water on his own. It just came naturally."

"Well, I think he's the best flier I've ever seen. Celeste is pretty good too. I'm so glad that you always tell me about them when we visit. It's more fun to know who I'm watching." Marina paused thoughtfully. "You know Eli, I think your dragons are the best of all," she said with the admiration of a proud little sister.

Eli's voice softened. "Thanks, but you know they are not exactly *my dragons*. I think I belong more to them."

"I know. I just meant the group you're training."

Eli led Marina to a wide, flat rock where they could enjoy the warmth of Zimzor's two suns. Marina listened with rapt attention as Eli recounted for her his most recent adventures in dragon training. Much to Marina's delight the serpentine neck of the young Roan bent down to rest his head on the warm rock beside her.

Their morning slipped quickly into afternoon. Marina bravely, yet cautiously reached out and placed her hand on Roan's head. His emerald green eyes opened briefly to gaze at his new companion before closing back into dragon sleep.

"Marina, I hate to say this, but you'd better get back before Mom gets home. She'll worry if she doesn't find you there. Let me talk to Zelina and then I'll walk you home. I don't want you climbing all the way back over the cliffs."

"I'll take her." Roan's head rose to look Marina in the eyes as he spoke to Eli. "She can just climb on my back and I'll fly Marina back to her watching spot."

Marina's eyes danced with delight at the thought of such a privilege.

"I don't know," Eli hesitated. "What if she falls off?"

"Don't worry, Eli. I'm sure Roan will fly slowly and very carefully for me," Marina bargained, "and I'll hold on tight!"

"She's right, Eli" came Zelina's voice from above on the cave path, "As you know, Marina won't be the first person ever to ride a dragon, just the youngest." She turned to Roan, "Now you take care, my young friend. This is a great responsibility to be given the opportunity to carry a person in flight."

So, after many promises for a gentle flight and

tight holding on, Marina climbed aboard Roan's back, seated herself in front of the spine just above his shoulders, leaned forward and stretched her arms as far around his neck as she could reach. Eli waved goodbye to his beloved little sister, feeling joy inside from her surprise visit. He kept a watchful eye as Roan made a graceful ascent and flew down the coast to the forest cliffs. He saw the young dragon make a delicate landing on the cliff peak, wait while Marina climbed down, then take off again, this time flying over the sea. Eli chuckled to himself at the boldness and bravery of his sister. If ever there was a devoted future dragon-keeper, Marina was it. She had more love for the dragons than anyone he knew. More, he thought, than some of the older dragon-keepers.

Mary Harrison

Chapter 12

Planning

"This one was tasty, better than the fish last night," Kane commented as he savored the flavor.

"Do you think it will come back?" Devon asked through a mouthful of berries.

"I'm sure it will. According to Father's legend, the dragons regularly patrol the coastline," concern was evident in her voice as Anaya answered. She absently stirred the berries in her shell with a finger.

"I think we need a plan. We've got to know

when the dragons come and when it is safe for us to hunt on the beach," Kane began as he thought out loud. "I think we should set up a watch. We'll take turns watching as lookouts from the cave entrance. Together we can find out the pattern of these patrols: times of day, number of dragons, how far they patrol, and if they ever land."

Both Devon and Anaya gasped at this last thought.

"For now, it seems to me the safest time to hunt and fish is soon after the dragons leave. We'll gather as many berries, sand animals and fish as we can. Then if we are unable to leave the cave for the remainder of the day, at least we'll have enough to eat."

Before long, life on the coast settled into a predictable routine. Kane, Devon and Anaya shared the daily watches at the cave entrance. They agreed that at first sight of a dragon, Anaya and Devon would seclude themselves at the back of the cave while Kane would lay flat behind the rocks at the entrance, peaking out to observe the dragon's movements.

They didn't have long to wait until their next sighting occurred. In the late afternoon it appeared as a faint black spot just above the horizon. Devon was taking the afternoon watch and quickly signaled his mother and Kane. He stayed with Kane a few minutes, watching the spot grow larger. First it swelled into a small black arch, and then

gradually grew into the shape of a body and large wings. Kane signaled Devon back into the cave as he lay down to observe.

Kane stifled a gasp as the dragon became clearer from his vantage point. It was huge and magnificent. The dragon's skin seemed to shimmer in the sunlight and radiated the most beautiful colors the boy had ever seen - blues, pinks, greens and lavenders. It was clearly a different dragon than the one he'd seen earlier. That one had been brown, blue and gray. Unbeknownst to Kane, he was watching Zonar, who often took his turn at the daily coastal patrols, as was the duty of all dragons.

Just as before the powerful dragon came from the south, made a graceful curve as it turned to follow the coast northward. Kane could feel the wind from its wings as the dragon passed their cave. It flew nearly out of sight, then turned and flew back towards the cave and beyond. Again, as they had witnessed earlier that day, the dragon made its patrol up and back down the beach, then headed back out to sea, gradually disappearing into the eastern horizon. Kane thought this dragon had flown lower than the dragon of the morning patrol.

As he rose and turned deeper into the cave, Kane realized that he was shaking. From fear? Perhaps a little. From amazement? Most definitely.

In hushed tones, although none of the three realized this, the small family discussed this latest dragon sighting and agreed that much more information was needed. Quickly, they set about gathering enough food for the evening meal. Anaya went picking in the berry thicket, Devon collected crabs from the rocks and sand while Kane set off to fish, hoping for more of the tasty red meat in the fish from the morning catch.

So much more to learn and to plan. Kane's thoughts wandered as he watched the tide for signs of fish. *They must have some kind of schedule. I wonder how many there are. I hope they're friendly - at least a little. Where do they live?* Kane's eyes focused out across the sea toward the horizon. The sea looked endless, yet the dragons came from somewhere beyond this endless water. *I've got to find out where. I must go there if we are to survive.*

So much more to learn and plan.

Mary Harrison

Chapter 13

Kane's Bold Plan Begins

Not long after Marina's surprise visit to Eli and the dragons, Kane awoke determined to explain his plan to Devon and their mother. The family had been living in the cave above the forbidden beach for some time now. Kane felt they had gathered enough information about the dragon patrols to begin the next step in his plan - a plan that he hoped would save their people.

The dragons patrolled the beach twice each day, around midmorning and again in the late

afternoon. Usually only one dragon made the patrol, although occasionally two flew together. At first the dragons stayed close to the coast, but in the last two weeks they often took a long flight over the forest as well. This made for a more dangerous situation on the beach, requiring the family to stay hidden in the cave longer each day. Kane was never sure how long the dragons would remain over the forest and they did not always return to the coast from the same direction as they embarked over the forest.

The tarkoza, Kane thought. *The dragons must be watching the tarkoza. Watching them eat our people.*

With these desperate thoughts Kane began his quest. Anaya handed him a bowl of berries and some smoked fish.

"We must make contact with them," Kane spoke slowly and cautiously, watching for her reaction.

"Contact with whom, son?" Anaya responded as she worked.

Devon's eyes widened, "With the dragons?"

"Yes. It's our only hope of saving our people."

"Saving our people! I'm more interested in saving our family. I will not have you putting yourself or your brother in that kind of danger. You have no idea what these dragons will do to you." Anaya's voice rose in desperation.

"Mother," Kane spoke quietly now, but with great conviction, "I know exactly what the tarkoza will do if they find us here. I saw what they did to Nantell's sons and I can't let that happen to our family. According to legend, the dragons came to the aid of the people across the sea when they were threatened by our ancestors."

"That's right, and ever since then we have been kept away from those people by the dragons. That makes us enemies. What makes you think they might help us now?"

"They must have some sense of compassion. Our people are in dire need now. Perhaps I can convince the dragons to come to our aid if we promise to remain on this side of the sea and leave the people across the sea alone in peace."

"He's right, Mother," Devon added his thoughts in a wavering voice. "We can't just hide in this cave forever. The dragons are our only hope."

The debate continued. Eventually, Anaya conceded that the boys were right. They must do something and they needed help to do anything. It appeared that the dreaded dragons were the only source of help available. In truth, it was the only option.

~ ~ ~

After lengthy explanation of his plan, Kane set off down the beach with Devon. Their goal was to gather as much of the larger pieces of driftwood as possible. Together they piled their supply of wood, tossed against the cliff base. Kane wanted the pile to look as if the tide had deposited it there. Meanwhile Anaya took the largest and strongest fur and began cutting it into long strips. It would only be a matter of days before Kane would use these to lash the logs together into a raft. In addition, food must be gathered, not only for the needs of each day, but enough to store for the dangerous journey across the sea.

~ ~ ~

Their work continued as days stretched into a week, then two. Kane and Devon caught more fish than the family could eat in a day. They kept Anaya busy cooking and drying the meat. Devon laid out berries to dry on the warm rocks. Keeping the cawing birds from stealing a free meal proved to be a difficult task, but Devon solved the problem by tying long leaves and vines onto thin branches. He then stuck his poles in the sand all around the drying fruit. These poles flapping in the breeze proved to be an effective deterrent to the birds. Kane made certain that the poles and fruit were moved before the dragon patrols each day. This task slowed their progress but could not be avoided.

As the work progressed, Kane continued to scan the sea, watching the waves and sky. No one in Kane's lifetime had ever sailed the sea. A few families made canoes and traversed the rivers of the forest, but those seemed quite small and gentle compared to this massive sea. Kane observed the region where the waves always crested and broke toward the shore. He selected a point midway between the rocky knoll to the south of their cave and the point of the cave entrance. Here the waters seemed calmer and there was plenty of space before the rocky knoll. The beach at this point was all soft sand. It was here that Kane would set off on his perilous journey.

As their plans progressed, Kane and his family saw the raft take shape, tightly lashed with strong leather strips. Mother said it was far too small, but Kane could only hide a raft of so much size from the daily dragon patrol. Kane crafted pegs and a driftwood box attached to the raft to hold his supplies. Meanwhile, Mother turned two smaller furs into bags for dried berries and fish. Devon sharpened two new spears for Kane's journey. And everyone watched the sky.

Mary Harrison

Chapter 14

Roan Joins the Dragon Patrol

Unbeknownst to Kane, one of the smaller dragons that he had seen on some of the recent two-dragon patrols had often been none other than Roan. As Eli had extended his training, Roan had naturally taken to longer and more arduous flights over the sea. In a matter of only a week since their race game, young Roan had become so confident over the water that he had been invited to join Dentax on his first training patrol clear across the sea.

Eli knew that Roan was ready for this arduous task. It was, after all, an honor for a dragon so young to be included in training patrols. Despite the honor, Eli felt a knot in his stomach as he watched his young charge fly off over the wide teal-blue sea. This was his first hatchling ever, his best friend among the dragons. He worried that the length of the flight might be too much for Roan.

"You've prepared him well, Eli." Tyffan's soft voice came from behind. "I've never seen any dragon-keeper train his charges with as much concern and dedication as you have. And Roan is the best young dragon that we've had in a long time. You've given so much confidence to him. I'm not sure how you did it but you've managed to teach him more sense and concern for people than any other young dragon has learned at his age." She gently squeezed his arm as she added, "Don't worry, he'll be fine. Dentax won't let anything happen to such a promising young dragon."

~ ~ ~

That first flight had been exhilarating for Roan. His eyes searched the vast sea below him. He knew they were following the path of Zimzor's twin suns to the west. Still, Roan felt sure he would loose his way without Dentax to guide him. The flight was long, but exciting none the less. Roan stretched his neck forward willing himself to see the goal ahead: the forbidden coast that was the ardent task of the dragons to patrol and protect from the vicious and war-like Jolaran hunters.

Then, there it was stretching before him on the horizon. The sight of the distant shore gave

Roan renewed strength just as he thought he had begun to tire. Flapping his wings harder, Roan pressed ahead of Dentax to get a better view.

And what a view it was as the two neared the coast! At first glance it looked much like the familiar coast on the Zimley side of the sea. Long stretches of sandy beaches, high rocky cliffs topped with dense forest. As the two drew nearer, Roan began to make out important differences. He saw no well traveled paths leading down to the beaches, only high, rugged cliffs. Here and there a few streams spilled down from the forest in small waterfalls, splashing on the rocks below. There were dark hollows between many of the rocks, caves according to Dentax, but they showed no signs of being occupied as were those in the dragon colony. Roan wondered at this, for his home in the caves always felt very comfortable and safe. He could not fathom a people who didn't want to use such wonderful caves for themselves. Why had the Jolarans not become coastal cave dwellers rather than fearsome forest hunters?

Dentax had kept that first patrol simple for Roan's sake. They soared in from the south and flew the distance of the beach, just as Kane was used to seeing. Far up the beach to the north out of Kane's sight, Dentax landed on a long sandy stretch of beach. Instructing Roan to rest there and do no exploring, Dentax winged his way over the forest. Not wanting to be gone for an extended period, Dentax briefly checked on the vicious progress of the tarkoza.

Dentax had returned to the beach from the northern part of the forest to find Roan drinking from a stream that tumbled over the cliffs. The young dragon seemed quite refreshed and ready for adventure. Roan, who had been studying the sea birds, cliffs and the edge of the forest above, was full of questions for the very experienced Dentax.

"Why don't the people here live in these wonderful caves? How do the same birds live on this side of the sea as the birds on our side of the sea? Can they fly clear across the sea like we do? Does the forest look as dense inland as it does from here? Is it dark in there?"

Dentax tipped his great serpentine head back and roared in laughter at the curiosity of this unique young dragon.

"Roan, you've spent too much time with Eli," he teased. "You're just like him. Eli always wants to know everything right away also! You sound just like Eli did when he first came to the dragon colony! Now, my little friend, we have news to take back to the dragon colony."

"News? What news?" Roan's natural curiosity was instantly peaked.

"It seems the tarkoza are still on the move. Their numbers still appear to be small, but we don't know that for certain. And we don't have any idea how many ravenously hungry young they can produce before they return to hibernation." Dentax explained the situation while he tried not to give Roan so much information as to frighten the youngster.

"I've heard the grown-up dragons taking about the tarkoza. They sound pretty vicious. Is Zonar going to have the dragon patrol help the Jolaran people?" Roan's innocence showed with this question.

"I don't know, Roan. For many generations the Zimley ranchers have provided our colony with all the meat we want in exchange for protection from their enemies, especially the Jolarans. We've become peaceful protectors rather than the hungry hunters we once were. To help the Jolaran people would upset the symbiotic balance we have with the Zimleys. Zonar knows that."

"But what if there are too many tarkoza? What happens to the Jolaran people then?" Roan persisted in his concern for the people across the sea.

"I don't know yet. Enough questions for now. It's time for us to head home. We wouldn't want that dedicated trainer of yours to worry about you being gone too long, now would we?"

"Oh, I hadn't thought about Eli worrying. You're right, Dentax, we better go."

Dentax only laughed more at Roan's concern for Eli as they took off down the beach for the last part of the morning patrol.

The return flight was uneventful and Roan thought about the many wonderful things he had to tell Eli and the others. He knew Celeste would want to hear all about the flight. She'd want to know if the forbidden coast was as beautiful as their coast. Celeste was always touched by the beauty of the world around them. Roan thought that was what made her such a special friend. He knew Eli liked that quality about Celeste as well. Eli told them that the beauty of the world was a gift from the Creator, to be cared for by those who dwell within its beauty.

Lost in his thoughts following Dentax home, Roan was surprised at how quickly the time seemed to pass. Before he knew it, his own coastal home was looming ahead on the horizon. His heart beat faster as he saw the dragon colony come into focus. Roan's eyes strained to see his friends.

And they were all there waiting, waving and cheering: Eli and Tyffan, Celeste and Zelina and the rest of the young dragons in the two training groups. Dentax landed with the grace of a seasoned flier. Roan was too excited and tripped as he touched down, but saved himself from completely rolling in a heap. No one seemed to notice as they all crowded around to congratulate him on his first patrol across the sea.

Chapter 15

Out to Sea

The morning finally arrived, clear and bright after the typical early morning mist over the sea lifted. Kane rose at dawn to prepare for his journey. He filled his water pouch from the stream that trickled down the cliff near the cave. Mother tied his bags of food tight and secure, and then stored them in the wooden supply box. Devon lashed down the new fishing spears while Kane added his wide driftwood paddle to the raft. He took only one sleeping fur, also tied down with care.

And then it was time. With tears in her eyes for a son she might never see again, Anaya gave Kane a hug. Kane placed Devon in charge of the family just as Father had placed him in charge not so long ago. Devon encircled Kane's waist with his arms in a hug that both boys never wanted to end.

"You take care of Mother for me now." Kane tousled Devon's hair as he spoke. "And save me some of those berries. I'll be back."

"I will. Well, no guarantee on the berries though. I might get hungry," Devon teased as the boys tugged the raft into the shallows of the tide.

With a smile and a wave far more confident than he felt, Kane took the raft from Devon and pushed it through the waves, deeper and deeper into the surf. Before he got to the point where the waves crested, Kane climbed aboard and began paddling. He had determined that he would have to cross this crucial point between crests. As he neared, Kane rode the raft over each wave, up and down, getting a feel for the raft and the constant movement of the sea.

Eyes scanning the horizon and the water building into the next wave, Kane saw his opportunity and paddled hard. He pushed himself, concentrated, and leaned into each stroke. Before he realized it, he had done it! He was past the breaking point! He could see the waves building behind him, not ahead.

With a shout of success, Kane turned back to the beach. He could see Mother and Devon waving and cheering his triumph. They looked so tiny from and so far away. Kane suddenly felt very small and alone. But he quickly pushed these feelings out of his mind and bravely waved back, shouting his goodbye.

Not forever, Kane reminded himself. *I'll see them again soon - with help.*

With that Kane, turned his attention to the sea before him. East. He must watch the sun and direct the raft – east, to the forbidden lands beyond the sea. To the people that were the Jolarans enemies. To the dragons - those huge and terrible dragons.

Mary Harrison

Chapter 16

Roan's Unexpected Find

In the next several weeks, Roan became much more comfortable and confident with the dragon patrols. He had now flown with several of the adult dragons and on this day he was flying with Zonar himself! As the two set off across the sea for the morning patrol, Zonar explained to Roan that he must learn to patrol over the forest, as the forest contained great danger that the dragons were watching. Roan remembered when Dentax told him about these terrible beasts on his first flight across

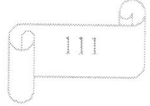

the sea. He listened intently as Zonar described the tarkoza, cautioning Roan not to fly too low and be caught by one of these vicious beasts. Roan was instructed not to make contact with any Jolaran people he might see, just report their condition to Zonar.

Together the two dragons approached the south beach. Roan flew low over the beach near the caves. Devon had taken up the watch from the cave entrance ever since Kane's departure. He could see them coming: the largest dragon of all and there was that small and very beautiful dragon that had become his favorite to watch. The young chocolaty dragon flew so close to the cave entrance that Devon felt the wind from its wings on his face.

Holding his breath, Devon leaned around the rock just enough to watch this beauty fly off to the north. He wondered about Kane, gone for many days now on the sea. Had these two powerful dragons seen him? Was he still alive on the raft? What would happen to Kane if the dragons did see him on the sea? Devon shivered at these thoughts and focused his attention on the sight before him.

Roan followed Zonar over the forest with great care. His eyes scanned the dense foliage below him. Roan heard sounds that made his voice rumble in a deep and defensive roar, while his heart beat faster. A huge tarkoza roared below, followed by screams of terror and pain from several Jolaran people. Roan strained to see the source of the disturbance.

His eyes widened at the sight he beheld. A huge beast reared up on its hind legs, more than three times the height of any human he had ever seen. Its powerful body covered in dense blue fur did nothing to disguise the rippling of enormous muscles. The head, though smaller than Roan expected, was still large and imposing with a mouth filled with the largest fangs Roan had ever seen. In its paws the tarkoza held a squirming, screaming human.

"Zonar, what can we do? Shouldn't we help him?" Roan pleaded.

Zonar shook his head as he answered, "Not now, it is not our place to rescue these people. That would defy our alliance with the Zimleys. We can't break that. Not yet."

Roan did not understand, but obeyed his leader. Shivering at the scene he had witnessed, Roan turned and followed Zonar over the forest, back to the coast. The two flew in silence as they headed back out to sea toward home.

It was from within his silent thoughts that Roan jerked back to concentration and focus. He had seen something, he was sure of it.

"What was that?" he asked. "I think I saw something."

"What did you see? I did not notice anything."

"Something was floating on the water."

"Probably just some drift wood. Fallen trees from the forest often float across the sea. It was nothing."

"I'd like to go back and make sure, if you don't mind sir," Roan remembered to be polite as he made his request. "I think it might have been someone."

"All right, if it will make you feel better, but I saw no person in the water. Make a quick survey and find out what you saw. You may return to the coast on your own."

Zonar had no desire for delay. His concern was great over the scene the dragons had witnessed in the forest. He must immediately convene a dragon council meeting upon his return.

"Report your findings to Eli when you return," Zonar instructed, confident that Roan would find nothing of importance.

Grateful for the opportunity, Roan turned and circled back the way they had come. His eyes scanned every inch of the sea below. Thinking he had been mistaken, Roan was about to turn back when he saw it. A tiny speck bobbed in the water below.

Roan descended for a closer look. There below, on a small raft of only a few logs, sat a boy about the same size as Eli. A very terrified boy. The boy held up a spear as if trying to frighten Roan away. Two of the friendly and always curious ocean dortles circled the raft as if protecting the floating boy. Roan could see that the boy trembled as he tried to look brave.

"You don't have to be afraid. I won't hurt you," Roan offered the only comfort he could think of.

"You can speak!" Kane had never imagined the dragons could speak, and even his language at that.

"Of course I can speak. All dragons speak. What did you expect?"

"I-I-I don't know. W-w-what are you going to do to me?" Kane managed to ask. He trembled, waiting for the answer from this small beauty. Despite his fear, Kane marveled at Roan's chocolaty-pink colors. He remembered seeing this one from his lookout at the cave entrance. *Perhaps his colors will change as he grows.*

"I'm not sure," Roan answered truthfully and

![illustration]

broke the spell of Kane's wondering. He had never imagined actually finding a person. Zonar had been so certain against the possibility. Now the inexperienced dragon debated this predicament as he circled the raft.

"Why are you floating on the sea?" Roan

thought he needed more information before choosing a course of action.

So this was it. Kane had hoped to make contact and now he had. The first dragon he met now wanted to know what he was up to. Fear welled up within him. *I could tell him I was on a raft in the river searching for food. My raft washed out to sea and I just got lost.* Kane trembled as he considered his words with care. He bravely decided the truth was the only thing to say.

"I'm looking for help. My people are being eaten alive by vicious beasts and we need your help if we are to survive." Kane stood on the raft, shivering as he spoke to the circling dragon.

"I know. I saw the beasts for the first time today. Zonar seemed very concerned, but he said we couldn't help the ones we saw today. Not yet, he said."

Roan thought about his last statement.

"Not yet. Hmmmm. Maybe he's planning something. He wouldn't have told me... I'm still in training." Roan's frustration became evident in his voice. Kane watched in silence as the young dragon debated with himself over what to do.

"I know!" Roan was suddenly excited with a new idea. "I'll take you to Eli. He always knows what to do."

Without waiting for a response, Roan swooped down and gently plucked Kane from the raft in his front claws. The dortles barked in surprise while Kane squirmed, filled with complete terror.

"Hold still. I don't want to drop you," Roan instructed as he swiveled his head down to look Kane in the eye. Looking down at the friendly dortles, Roan spoke words of assurance. "Don't worry, I won't hurt him. I've carried a person in flight before… although she rode on my back." Then looking back to Kane, he added, "I can't land on the water to let you climb on, so I'll just have to carry you this way. I'll be careful."

Kane took a deep breath and tried to relax and hold still. He felt the wind in his face pick up as Roan ascended and winged harder to the east.

"Do you have a name?" Kane shouted over the wind.

"I'm called Roan. What about you?"

"Kane, my name is Kane. Who is Eli?"

"He's my trainer. You'll like him," Roan answered with pride. After that the two were silent for the remainder of the return flight.

As Roan expected, Eli was waiting for his return. He looked worried, probably because Zonar had returned without him.

Roan made a graceful arc as he approached the beach and gently deposited a windblown and frightened Kane at Eli's feet. He landed beside the boys and smiled at Eli, as if he had just presented Eli with the greatest of gifts.

Mary Harrison

Chapter 17

Sorting out the Truth

Eli looked from Kane to Roan and back. "Roan, I don't understand. Who is this?"

"His name is Kane," Roan smiled as he introduced the boys. "Kane this is my trainer and best friend, Eli."

"Nice to meet you, Kane." Eli continued to look from one to the other.

"Roan, you've got some explaining to do. Where did you find him?"

Roan began a careful account of his flight

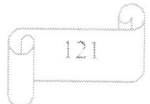

with Zonar over the forest, seeing the horrible tarkoza, then spotting something over the sea and seeking Zonar's permission to have another look.

"Well, at least that explains why Zonar returned without you. I was very worried. I thought something had happened to you."

"Zonar told me to report to you whatever I found, so here he is!" Roan ended with a triumphant smile.

"So you have. Now the question remains, what do we do next?" Eli thought aloud. Then turning to Kane, he asked, "Maybe I need to hear your story. Why were you on a raft in the sea? Traveling across the sea is forbidden to both the Jolarans and the Zimleys.... Wait. First we need to get you some dry clothes and something to eat. You look like something a baby dragon just dragged in." Eli grinned and winked at Roan.

Eli led Kane to his own personal dwelling cave and waited patiently while Kane cleaned up and changed clothes. Eli's clothes proved to be a good fit for Kane, even though he was a bit younger. Eli noted the strength apparent in Kane's muscles, a sign of a strong hunter. Eli was joined by Tyffan as he prepared a meal for Kane. She was as full of curiosity about their new arrival as Eli, so she stayed with the boys as Kane ate.

Feeling much better after his first warm and delicious meal since setting out to sea, Kane's confidence was somewhat restored. He knew it was time to recount the events of the last many months. Kane began by explaining the Jolaran way of life, with weaker families being driven off their hunting grounds. He described every detail he could remember of the tarkoza attack on Nantell's clan and the narrow escape of his own beleaguered family. He then described in a wavering voice how he and his mother and brother had been living on the forbidden coast in a cave above the beach. He even admitted to his careful observations of the dragon patrols, hunting for fish, clams and berries when the dragons left, and his plan to sail across the sea and seek help from the mighty dragons.

"I must present our plight to their leader. Roan said they have a leader and I must speak with him," Kane finished with a hopeful sigh as he waited for Eli to take it all in.

Eli rubbed his forehead as he tried to comprehend everything Kane had told him. The thought of an entire people being eaten periodically by hungry beasts whenever they awoke from hibernation was almost more than he could imagine. Eli had learned in history classes about the vicious hunters across the sea who had laid siege to the peaceful Zimleys many generations ago. It was a point of local pride that the dragons had come to the aid of the Zimleys, not the Jolarans, during their long conflict. The peace agreement between the Zimleys and the dragon colony had come from that time so long ago. Eli had always thought the

Jolarans were their enemies, but now he questioned whether this was really true. It seemed to Eli that the tarkoza were the true enemy in this situation.

"You're right, Kane, we must go to Zonar. He has convened the dragon council and keepers are not allowed inside the meeting cave. But your situation is desperate and we need to seek permission to join this meeting." Eli looked hard at Kane, "We could be thrown out of the dragon colony or even killed if Zonar is angered by our intrusion. Are you willing to take that risk?"

"I have risked the lives of my family to be here. I must take that risk, otherwise there is no hope for my people," came Kane's firm and resolute response.

Eli smiled; glad to have made such a brave new friend.

Mary Harrison

Chapter 18

A Dangerous Meeting

Eli led the way through the labyrinth of caves that formed the dragon colony, twisting back and forth many times. Roan followed a safe distance behind, for he knew that he was far too young a dragon to be allowed in the great council meeting. At last they came to the largest cave deep within the mountainous cliffs. Here all the eldest dragons were in attendance at Zonar's command. Eli, Kane and Tyffan heard their deep voices rumbling in debate inside. A single shiver seemed to run through all three youths at once. Eli took a deep breath and headed for the opening.

Zelina was seated very near the entrance, observing from the mouth of the meeting cave. As Eli and the others approached, their movement caught her eye. Zelina turned her long neck toward them and poked her head out to meet the trio. She blinked in surprise as her eyes focused on Kane, then looked over his head to see a sheepish Roan ducking his head behind Kane in a futile effort to hide from her gaze.

"Eli, what are you doing here, and who is this? You know you're not supposed to be near the meeting cave during a dragon council. Even so, you've brought a visitor, which is also forbidden," Zelina accused Eli, hardly able to believe that her prized young keeper would dare to break such an immutable law of the colony.

"He's not just any visitor. Roan found him. Zonar let Roan go back to check on something he saw on the sea during their return flight this afternoon. He was told to report his findings to me. Roan did more than that - he brought him to me!

"This is Kane. He's a Jolaran seeking help from the dragon colony. I suspect that Kane's need for help is exactly what Zonar and the others are discussing. We come to ask permission to speak with the council. Zonar and the others need to hear Kane's story." Eli waited, holding his breath as Zelina pondered his plea to be heard. She seemed to understand, for Zelina nodded her immense head and turned back inside, toward the council leaders. She waited patiently for a break in the conversation.

"Zonar, Great Leader of our colony," Zelina bowed her head in respect as she spoke, gaining the attention of all the dragons present. "Hear me, I beg you. I have just been made aware that there is more information available about the situation with the Jolarans and the tarkoza than that observed by our patrols."

"More information?" questioned Zonar's deep rumbling voice. "How is this possible? All the recent patrol dragons are present and we have heard all of their observations."

"All but one, for you left Roan to check on something upon the sea and told him to report his findings to Eli. He's done that and more. Roan found something that you must all see…and hear." Zelina's mouth curved in a smile as she imparted this news. "Eli and Roan are here to present you with this new information."

"Very well, bring them in."

There was a collective gasp from the dragon elders as Eli, followed by Kane and Roan stepped

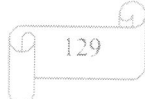

inside the meeting cave. No one seemed to notice that Tyffan had followed the small group inside. Murmurs and questions resounded throughout the cave.

"Enough!" Looking from Eli to Kane, then to Roan and back, Zonar shook his head.

"Is this what you found, Roan, a boy?"

"Yes sir," Roan managed to remember to bow his head to their king, and then looked up grinning wide over his great discovery. "He was floating on some wood. I brought him to Eli, just as you told me to."

"Hmm. Well, I did tell you to report to Eli, although I never actually said to bring him whatever you found." Zonar's eyes sparkled at Roan as he spoke. "You've done well, my little friend. You have proven yourself to be a worthy member of the dragon patrol."

Roan beamed, speechless.

Then turning his attention to Kane, Zonar addressed him. "What is your name, please?"

"Kane….s..s..sir,"

"You have nothing to fear, Kane. We dragons are peaceful and you are safe within these caves. I see you are wearing Eli's clothes. Has he taken good care of you since your arrival?" Zonar attempted to make the boy feel more at ease before they went any further.

"Why, y-y-yes. Eli has been very kind. Tyffan, too," Kane stammered.

"Good, good, we always want our keepers to do their best to care for everyone and anyone in the colony. Now, Kane, tell me, from where did you come…before the sea, that is," Zonar's eyes were steady and met Kane's as he waited for the answer he already knew.

"I am from the forests of Jolara," Kane began. "My people are in desperate need of help. The forests are filled with horrible beasts. We call them tarkoza. They have only recently awakened from hibernation and are killing and eating our people. If any of us are to survive, we need help. It was…is my hope that the powerful dragons that patrol our coast may be willing to come to our aid."

Zonar's eyes narrowed. "What do you know of the dragon patrols?" he asked with more than simple curiosity in his voice.

Kane gulped. So this was it, time to confess his secret observations and plans. Taking a deep breath, Kane answered, "My family and I were driven from our hunting grounds just before the tarkoza attacked. I saw what they did to the hunters who took our land. The sight shot terror through my heart. So, I took my mother and brother and made our way through the forest to the south and east – to the coast. We have been living in a cave above the beach since then. We watch the dragon patrols every day from inside the cave - to find out when you come and how many and where you go. Once we had a pretty good idea of when to expect you, my brother and I built a raft and I set out to sea to find you. Will you help us?"

Silence filled the enormous cave at this revelation of Jolarans carefully observing the dragon patrols. No one dared speak. Then Zonar roared in laughter, shaking his long serpentine neck with abundant joy.

"Oh, I see we have another dragon watcher in

our midst. It seems Marina is not the only one brave enough to sneak a glimpse of our routines, no matter how forbidden," the gleam had returned to Zonar's eyes. "You are a courageous young man, Kane. And resourceful, too, secretly keeping watch while caring for your family's safety.

"Well now, what are we going to do about this new evidence? This meeting is because of our knowledge of the plight of the Jolarans. It is clear only the most resourceful Jolarans may survive the current awakening of the tarkoza. Yet we are restricted from aiding them because of our peace agreement with the Zimleys," Zonar looked around the cave. All eyes were on him, waiting for his decision.

"Kane, where is your family now?"

"I left them on the beach. Devon will continue to catch fish and gather berries for our mother. They agreed to remain in the safety of the cave until I return with help."

"Hmmm. How long were you on the raft?"

"Eight days, sir; today was the ninth morning when Roan found me."

"We'd better not keep them waiting any longer. I'm certain they are worried about you." *And I hope they're still alive,* Zonar finished his thought silently.

"Dentax, take Rosamae and Tremor over to the Jolaran coast. Set up a watch on the beach. Determine which cave this boy's family is hiding in without frightening them too much. Keep them safe, Dentax," Zonar's orders got swift obedience as the dragons left.

Turning to Zelina, Zonar gave his next orders. "Get the saddles - four of them. It's been a very long time since we have used the saddles. Do you remember how to handle them, Zelina? We don't want anyone slipping off over the sea."

"Of course I remember, Zonar. The human safety saddles were my specialty once, you know," Zelina answered with a note of pride.

"Good. Zelina, I want you along on this flight. You may choose the other dragons who will accompany you," Zonar finished.

Kane listened while Zonar gave his orders which seemed to be understood by the dragons. He, however, was quite confused.

"Wait! What are you doing? You can't just go and capture my family. I know we're not supposed to be living on the forbidden coast. But it was the only way I could see to survive. You can't hurt them," Kane pleaded.

"Hurt them? Nobody said anything about hurting your family, Kane. We are going to rescue them. Kane, it is clear to me that you are a brave young man who cares about his family and the safety of his people. Despite the warnings about the forbidden coast, you have searched for the only possible source of help. I believe you are a heartfelt seeker of the Creator's truth and guidance," Zonar spoke calmly to reassure him. "Now, I want you and Eli to have Zelina secure each of you on one of those saddles. I think your mother might be more willing to climb aboard a dragon if she sees you on one first! I really don't want her frightened too badly."

"Rescue them? Not capture them?" A wave of relief flooded over Kane. "Oh, thank you, Zonar!"

Turning to Eli, Zonar continued, "Pay close attention as Zelina gets the saddles set for you. You'll need to hook Kane's family in the safety straps on each saddle. Be sure the straps are tight to keep them from falling. Bring them back here to the dragon caves."

Then looking at the still very quiet Tyffan, Zonar instructed her to prepare a guest cave for their soon-to-arrive visitors.

"There is much to do and the council must decide how to proceed next," Zonar finished as he turned his attention back to the dragon council members.

Chapter 19

Rescue

Zelina hurried to retrieve the saddles from within the supply caves. She returned to Eli and Kane with a gleam in her eyes, anticipating this great adventure they were embarking upon. Swiftly, Zelina donned the first saddle, cinching it snuggly, but not too tight, at the base of her thick neck slightly in front of her shoulder, just right to position a rider. Her front paws, more hand-like than not, deftly demonstrated to Eli the correct manner for a human rider to be secured. Once confident that Eli could make the necessary adjustments to keep each rider safe, Zelina turned to the small group around her.

"Eli, you'll ride with me. Kane, I want you on Galen." Zelina nodded to a huge golden dragon.

Kane recognized this dragon from the patrols and was certain he had been in the meeting cave earlier. Taking a deep breath, Kane went over to Galen and nodded his understanding.

"Now Kane, tell me about your brother. What is his age and how large is he?" she asked.

"Devon is eight-years-old and about this tall," Kane gestured. "He's rather small and thin for his age."

"Roan, do you think you can make another flight across the sea today?" Zelina looked at the young dragon waiting with great anticipation.

"Oh, yes! Absolutely," Roan replied with delight.

"Then you shall carry Kane's younger brother. Very carefully, just like you did Marina," Zelina instructed. "Lastly we need someone to carry the boys' mother." Her eyes scanned the small group assembled and watching their preparations. Zelina's gaze stopped at Celeste.

"I think you are ready for this great task, young one. You, too, have proved yourself capable on recent dragon patrols. "

Celeste bowed her head in respect. "Thank you for your confidence in me, Zelina. I will carry the woman with great care."

With the selections made, the remaining preparations went smoothly and with impressive speed. The harnesses were secured on the remaining three dragons. Tyffan brought packs with food and water for the travelers and the family they planned to rescue.

Kane climbed aboard Galen and waited while Eli secured the straps on his saddle. This would be the second time in a day, his first day of actually meeting the dragons, when he would be carried across the sea by one of these tremendous beasts. Kane felt safer than he had earlier, but a tremor of fear still rose up from within.

No fear. I must not dwell this. Fear won't help Mother and Devon. I won't fall. Kane tried to reassure himself while working very hard not to show his fear to the others in the group.

Eli finished securing his own safety straps on the saddle aboard Zelina. He and Kane each carried a pack of supplies. One final preparation remained. Zelina handed the boys each weapons – just in case - a spiked club for Kane and a spear with multiple points to Eli. The four dragons left the caves and

walked down to the beach with the small group of admiring training dragons watching them. Then, with a nod from Zelina, they were off.

~ ~ ~

Eli had never felt such exhilaration! The wind in his face. The view as the twin suns sparkled on the vast sea below. The strength and power of Zelina as she winged her way west. Eli leaned to his right, allowing himself a better forward view. He wanted to see the Jolaran coast as soon as possible. A short time later, it came into view. First, it was just a thin line on the horizon, but soon became an ever growing land. It was not long before Eli could make out the shoreline, rocky cliffs and the dense forest towering above.

As the group flew on in silence, Eli suddenly sat up straighter and strained to see movements on the beach where they were clearly heading. His heart pounded at the sights that gradually came into sharp focus. For there on the beach were indeed the three dragons sent to protect Kane's family. To the north of the trio lumbered a huge, shaggy blue beast. The tarkoza had found the beaches of Jolara at last!

Kane, too, had seen the beast. "Hurry, Galen," he called to his powerful mount.

As the group neared the beach, the gravity of

the situation became quite clear. Rosamae the largest of the female dragons, and Zonar's mate, reared on her hind legs, covering a cave entrance with her body. She blocked the entrance, keeping the humans inside from the hungry tarkoza. Dentax and Tremor formed a perimeter between Rosamae and the tarkoza. Dentax roared and reared up to his full height, swinging his front claws, threatening the approaching tarkoza. Tremor braced himself, crouched, ready to spring into battle any moment.

"Galen, look to the left! The cliffs just south of the cave entrance!" Kane called with desperate fear in his voice.

His call was unnecessary, for Galen had already seen it too. A small tarkoza made its way down the rocks just to the south of the cave.

"Try not to worry, Kane," Galen reassured, "I'm sure Rosamae has seen it too. She has a deep love for all humans and would die protecting that cave entrance. She'll back into that cave herself to protect them. Zonar knows this. That's why he sent his mate to your family."

Kane felt a bit awestruck at this revelation. Zonar, willing to place his own mate in danger to save his small, endangered family. Kane shook with a wave of relief. The dragons really could be trusted. They would help his people - starting with

Kane's own family.

"Zelina, I'll take care of that little one on the rocks. You three help Rosamae. We must hurry to get these people to safety," Galen called over to Zelina.

"Exactly as I was thinking."

"Kane, you'd better hold on tight," Galen's deep voice seemed much louder as he curved his neck around to address the boy. "The ride might be a bit rough for a while."

"Don't worry. I will," Kane replied. He tightened his hold on Galen's neck just below a sparkling spine and whispered a prayer of hope for his family.

With that, Galen broke from the rest of the group, made a wide and fast arch to the south. He swooped down from the sky behind the young tarkoza, attacking from the rear. Kane leaned left and raised his mace watching for opportunity to strike the beast. With a mighty blow from Galen's front paw, the tarkoza tumbled down the rocks, crashing to the beach.

The young beast was injured, alive and very angry. It rose on four shaggy blue feet, snarled at Galen and attempted to swipe a blow as the dragon swooped down for another pass. Galen was not to be outdone, however. He twisted sharply and laid a

thunderous blow from his tail alongside the head of the tarkoza. The small beast dropped to its side. Not knowing if the tarkoza was still alive, but before it had a chance to move again, Galen zoomed in a third time, leaned his long neck down and grabbed the tarkoza by the throat. He raised it just enough to give the animal a firm shake. Hearing the neck snap, Galen dropped the limp beast back on the beach.

Heart racing and body trembling, Kane was grateful when Galen landed just below the cave entrance. Galen had been right about Rosamae. She was on the ledge, her tail backing into their cave to more thoroughly block the entrance.

"Kane, get down and go to your family," Zelina instructed with urgency.

Kane's hands were shaking too badly from the battle he and Galen had just waged. He was unable to release the clips on the saddle straps. Eli saw this, released himself and was aboard Galen's back helping Kane before Kane realized. Eli snapped the clips open and Kane was free. Both boys leaped from Galen's back and ran toward the cave.

Once the boys were off, Galen turned his attention to Dentax, Tremor and the much larger tarkoza. Together the three massive warriors surrounded the approaching and vicious animal. Deafening roars emanated from all three dragons, only to be matched by the screams of the angry beast. Dentax attacked first, striking a blow to its left shoulder. Tremor followed immediately with claws deep into the haunches. Galen again used his tail and went for the head. Each blow only seemed to anger the tarkoza more, for it showed no signs of backing off.

Meanwhile, the boys had climbed to the cave, squeezed past Rosamae and found Devon and their mother trembling at the back of the cave. Kane scooped his family into his arms. Both Anaya and Devon sobbed as the three embraced.

Eli waited a moment before he spoke. "Kane, we've got to hurry. I don't know how long the dragons can keep that thing away."

Kane nodded and tipped Anaya's face to meet his gaze. "Mother, I've brought help. The dragons have come to our rescue. Now, you've got to trust me that you're going to be all right. This is my friend, Eli. He's going to hook you up on a saddle….aboard a dragon. Then we're going to fly back across the sea."

"Really?" Devon's wide eyes peered up at Kane as the boys released their grip on each other.

"Yes, really."

"But Kane, are they safe? I didn't know who to be more afraid of, the dragons sitting on the beach or the tarkoza, so we tried to hide from them all," Anaya's voice trembled as she spoke. "Then this dragon jumped to our ledge and blocked the entrance. She spoke! I couldn't believe my ears!"

"I know, Mother, it is all quite amazing. But we must go now."

Kane gave his mother and Devon a refreshing drink and brief bit of food from his pack, then he and Eli ushered the family toward the entrance.

"Rosamae, you can let us out now," Eli called.

Rosamae gracefully jumped from the ledge and flew to join the others in battle. Zelina, Roan

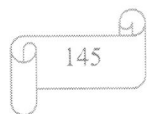

and Celeste waited just below the cave, ready to receive their riders. Eli helped Devon onto Roan's back and secured the straps as if he were a seasoned expert at the task. Next, Kane coaxed his mother onto Celeste's back and soothed her with gentle conversation while Eli fastened her in.

After Rosamae joined the fray against the tarkoza, Galen returned for Kane, who was quickly secured by Eli's deft hands. At last, Eli climbed back aboard his dear friend, Zelina, secure for the trip home. As the small group rose from the beach, Eli looked back to see the battling dragons attack the tarkoza at once. Claws and teeth from all three sank deep into the tarkoza. It gave up one last scream, convulsed in their grip, and then fell still. The first battle was won.

Tremor and Dentax both had wounds, but neither took any notice of them as the trio winged hard to catch up with the rest of the group heading home.

Home. Home to safety. Home to Zonar and hard decisions for the dragon council leaders.

Chapter 20

Safe at Last

The group of seven dragons and four humans could see a welcoming party on beach as they neared the refuge of the dragon colony. Tyffan and the two groups of young training dragons waited with great expectation on the beach while Zonar towered above them from his cave entrance. The little dragons cheered and flapped their wings as the weary travelers touched down. Eli slipped out of his harness as soon as Zelina's feet met the sand. He rushed to release Kane first. Both boys helped

Anaya safely down from Celeste's curving back. They were met by Tyffan who offered a supporting arm and a warm smile to the shaking woman.

Devon seemed much less in a rush to dismount. He leaned forward and hugged Roan's neck. "You're my favorite dragon of all, Roan," the boy spoke quietly. The two had shared more than just introductions during the flight across the sea.

"Wow, why's that?" Roan couldn't hide his surprise.

"From the very first time I saw you patrolling our coast, I've watched for you to come back. You are the most beautiful of all the dragons. I know someday you're going to be huge and as powerful as any of the larger dragons," Devon spoke with pride the thoughts he had kept secret during the long days of watching and waiting. "I'm glad you're my friend now."

Roan could only smile as he turned neck and lowered his head to gently rub against Devon's tousled hair.

By the time Devon's feet were firmly on the ground, Zonar had joined the others on the beach. He tenderly rubbed his forehead against that of Rosamae, grateful for the safe return of his beloved mate. Zonar congratulated each of the dragons, Eli and Kane on completing their dangerous mission.

With concern, he took note of Dentax's and Tremor's wounds. He dispatched them to their caves for rest and sent for keepers to tend the wounds sustained by the heroes of the moment.

Turning to Kane's mother, Zonar addressed her, "Welcome to our colony. What is your name?"

"Anaya," her voice wavered as she leaned on Kane for support. The events of the day were all a bit much for such a timid woman.

"Anaya, you must be very proud of your son. He has bravely sought our help against great odds. The dragon patrol is very well aware of the plight of your people. As king, I tell you that I am willing to risk our long standing peaceful alliance with the Zimleys in order to come to your aid," Zonar smiled as he reassured her. "We will discuss the details further after you have rested."

Tyffan then led the small group to the waiting cave she had prepared, complete with clean, dry clothes for everyone in Kane's family, comfortable beds made ready for their rest and a hearty, hot meal. Eli and Tyffan then left the small family alone to enjoy their respite together now that they were safely reunited.

Mary Harrison

Chapter 21

Eli's Message

Back outside, Eli and Tyffan heard Zonar's deep voice summoning the dragons to another council meeting. They watched as all the great dragons made their way up the path, through the caves toward the meeting cave. At last, Zonar and Rosamae followed the others inside. Pausing at the cave entrance, Zonar looked back and addressed the pair of young keepers.

"Eli and Tyffan, you are as much a part of this now as any of the dragons. Please join us. And

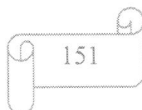

bring Roan and Celeste along as well."

Unable to hide their surprise or pleasure, Eli and Tyffan turned to follow them up the path. Glancing over his shoulder, Eli took note of Roan and a very quiet Celeste joining the procession.

Once inside, Zonar's rumbling voice called for order. "Rosamae and Zelina will first share with us the events of today's rescue."

Silence settled throughout the cave as the two female dragons recounted the sight of the tarkoza on the beach as the rescue party arrived. They shared details of the younger tarkoza climbing down the cliffs toward the cave, Galen's swift defeat of that one, then the arduous battle against the much larger tarkoza.

When last accounts had been finished, no on spoke and all eyes turned on Zonar.

"As you know, earlier today the council leaders all agreed that we must inform the Zimleys of the plight of their Jolaran brothers and of our decision to intervene," Zonar began with great firmness and resolution in his voice. "The Jolarans have as much right to live and enjoy a peaceful existence as the Zimleys. It is our belief that the Creator meant for all people to live equally in peace and safety. It is also clear that ever since the first tarkoza tasted human flesh, these beasts have become the embodiment of evil with an unrelenting thirst for blood. We will address the Zimley council leaders regarding this grave situation. My plan is to do everything we can to keep our peaceful coexistence with the Zimleys in place, while at the same time developing a protector relationship with the Jolarans."

Turning to Eli, Zonar continued, "You must contact your father.   Tell him to call a meeting of the Zimley Council first thing in the morning. Let him know the dragons will be in attendance."

Eli nodded and gulped at the same time. In his entire youth, he could recall many days watching the dragons fly gracefully over town and even seeing their flights over the sea. But aside from the time he witnessed his father's swearing in, Eli never heard of the dragons attending a council meeting. He was as committed to the safety of Kane and his people as Zonar, so Eli knew for certain he would do just as Zonar instructed.

After the meeting, Eli found Roan sleeping at the back of the meeting cave, exhausted from two trips across the sea. Quite a task for such a tender, youthful dragon, but a day Eli knew that Roan would never have wanted to miss. He gently shook Roan to wake him; just enough to guide the sleepy dragon back to his own cave. Together, Eli and

Tyffan fed all the young dragons in their two groups. Then, without another word, Eli slipped out of the cave and down to the beach. There he found Galen waiting for him.

"Thanks for waiting for me, Galen," Eli began as he walked toward the golden giant. "I just had to take care of my group. I feel that I have neglected most of them today."

"Today it was necessary. Besides, I'm sure Tyffan looked out for your charges while we were gone. She's just as dedicated a keeper as you are," Galen reassured him. "Now we must be off to your family. You have a message to deliver."

In what seemed like a brief moment, Galen had flown Eli over the forest cliffs and landed on the beach on the Zimley side of the forest. The two stopped to pick up Marina from her watching spot, as today was the end of her school week.

"I'll wait here for you," Galen told the two as they turned toward the path leading to town.

Eli and Marina waved and hurried toward town. Marina, who had seen the return flight with the human passengers, was filled with questions. So Eli filled her in on the walk toward their parents' home. Eli noted how strange it was to be going "home" after so long in the dragon colony. He had long ago come to consider the colony his home.

"Dragons at the council meeting!" Marina's eyes widened in surprise. "I've never heard of dragons actually coming into town. Come to think of it, today when Galen landed on our beach is the first time I've ever seen a dragon land on our side of the forest. This is really serious!"

Before he realized it, Eli and Marina were at their parents' door. He cautioned Marina not to share any details with their parents yet. Then Eli stopped to knock.

"No silly, we live here, remember?" Marina giggled as she went inside. "Mom, Dad, we're home," she called.

"We? Who's we?" Clarice called from the kitchen. "Go wash up, Marina, dinner is just about ready."

"Hi, Mom," Eli spoke softly.

Clarice's great surprise at seeing her son at home after such a long, though honorable, absence brought her over to smother Eli in the warmth of her hugs and kisses. Before long, Eli pulled himself away and looked at his mother with a serious determination in his eyes.

"Where is Dad?" Eli asked.

"In his study going over some new laws the council is considering,"

"I have come to speak with him. I bring a

message from the dragon council."

Clarice quieted and looked at Eli with deep concern. She allowed him to go to her husband and deliver his message alone. She pulled Marina close.

"I wonder what that is all about," she spoke aloud to herself.

"Eli said I can't tell anyone. He has to tell Dad, then Dad has to tell the council," Marina answered their mother in a quiet voice.

~ ~ ~

"Hi, Dad. So how's life with the new position? Do you like serving on the town council?" Eli asked as he walked into this father's private study.

"Eli! What are you doing here? It's so good to see you. Yes, I like my work quite well these days," Dawson rose to greet Eli and give him a hug and handshake. "And what about you, son? Getting tired of the dragon colony, are you?"

Eli smiled at his dad's teasing. Dawson knew that Eli would never tire of working for the dragons. "I've come to deliver a message. Zonar needs your assistance with a matter for the town council. He wants you to call a meeting of all the council leaders first thing in the morning. There is a serious situation that the dragons will discuss with our leaders."

"First thing in the morning? That's pretty short notice, Eli, but I'll see what I can do," Dawson responded in disbelief. "It is most unusual for the dragons to call us to a meeting in this manner."

"I know that, Dad. But this is a very serious

situation."

"Maybe if you could give me some of the details it would make it easier to convince the council members to convene on such short notice - and at the demand of the dragons," Dad pried for more information.

"Sorry, that's for Zonar to discuss, not me. I'm just the messenger," Eli responded, resolved not to divulge any more than Zonar had instructed.

"Well, I don't know about this. It's most unusual. I'll try, at least I'll see what I can do," came Dawson's reply.

"No Dad, you must do more than try. Make it happen! You must," Eli was firm, and could hardly believe himself talking to his own father this way. "The situation cannot wait another day. Tomorrow. First thing in the morning," Eli paused and gazed into his dad's eyes. "I have to get back to the colony. Galen's waiting." Eli turned to leave.

Stopping by the kitchen, Eli gave his mom a goodbye hug before leaving. He chose not to stay for dinner in order to avoid a conversation that might cause him to divulge anything about the Jolarans. Walking down the path toward the beach, Eli turned to wave one last time at Marina and Clarice. He saw his dad watching from the study window.

Make it happen. The situation cannot wait another day. Whatever could be so wrong at the dragon colony to warrant demanding this meeting? Dawson pondered the situation as he watched his son leave.

Mary Harrison

Chapter 22

The Great Debate

The day dawned clear and bright with a glorious sunrise as the twin suns broke over the horizon. Eli stretched as he rose, eager to get his morning duties completed caring for his group of juvenile dragons. He had hardly slept, his mind racing all night with thoughts of the remarkable meeting that would take place this very day.

Eli met Tyffan as the two prepared the morning meal for their dragons.

"I'm going to that meeting today," Eli

confessed in a hushed voice as he prepared a haunch of beef to serve Roan.

"I know," Tyffan replied. "And I'm going with you."

The two shared a long moment of silence, looking deep into each others eyes.

"What do you think will happen when our people find out?" Tyffan asked.

"I'm not sure. I know that my father was not all that happy about being summoned to a meeting by the dragons. I think the council may take a lot of convincing about this. Remember how much pride there is in town over the dragons protecting us and not the Jolarans?"

"I think if some of the keepers are there to share what we've have seen, it might help," Tyffan offered her thoughts.

Nodding his agreement, Eli worked quickly to finish his morning tasks.

~ ~ ~

Outside on the dragons' beach, the dragon council members were gathering when Eli and Tyffan came down the path. Zonar and Rosamae led the group of massive leaders down the beach a short distance. Dentax and Tremor's wounds had been carefully tended and were already beginning to heal. Galen's golden scales sparkled in the morning sun. Zelina had harnesses in her front claws. The other eldest dragons, Handrill, Jorno, Sylvie and Chesmare all gathered round, awaiting Zonar's instructions.

"We will conduct this meeting in the Zimley town square. I expect it may not be easy to get Master Oliver and the others to hear our case for aiding the Jolarans," Zonar explained as Eli and Tyffan joined the group. "We will need to bring Kane and Anaya along to tell their story. Galen, I want you to keep careful watch over them." Turning to Eli, Zonar continued, "You and Tyffan will also be joining us. Tyffan, go now and see if Kane and his mother are ready. Find Roaul while you're inside. He can entertain Devon while his mother is gone. Perhaps give the boy a tour of the dragon colony. I think he'd like that."

Tyffan smiled as she set off. Zonar was always so considerate to the humans that lived in his colony. *What a privilege it is to work among these powerful beasts*, Tyffan thought as she climbed the rocky path.

"Eli, I want you to bring Roan and Celeste to the meeting as well," Zonar said. "I want to show the Zimleys that even our youngest patrol dragons are willing to participate in saving these people."

"I'll get them right away," Eli responded

quickly as he bounded back up the rocks. His heart filled with pride, knowing that his two young charges were once again selected for a great honor. He was so proud of both of them after yesterday's rescue.

In short order the group was ready to leave. Eli, Tyffan, Kane and Anaya slipped onto saddles aboard their waiting dragon friends. Today Kane smiled at the waiting Galen, no sense of fear remaining. He knew he was safe aboard his golden giant. With a brief nod from Zonar, the group rose as one. Powerful wings beat and gracefully swooped over the forest toward the town of Zimley.

~ ~ ~

Marina gazed out the window, bored with her studies in mathematics. She knew the path she wanted her life to take and doubted that it would require much of the advanced mathematics she now studied. She had never heard Eli talk about using his math skills at the dragon colony. Marina imagined herself making that momentous walk down the path which only the leaders were allowed to take, and then only on rare occasions; the path to the dragon colony.

Her mind's eye could see her beloved friends soaring above the town, over the forests and out over the water of the great sea. Marina daydreamed

of riding Roan over the forest again someday. She suddenly snapped back to attention as her eyes focused on the sights outside her class window. Soaring downward and across the lawn of the school flew dragons! No less than twelve of them! Marina had never seen so many dragons over the town before. And they were landing! Right in the middle of the town square! Marina watched as all twelve dragons set down gracefully, folded their wings and looked to Zonar for instructions. Marina knew that her eyes were not fooling her when she recognized Eli and three other people aboard four of the dragons.

"Look," Marina burst out, "the dragons are in the town square!"

The class of twelve year old students forgot all about their math studies as everyone hurried to the window. Amid chattering students wondering what was going on a boy's voice rose: "Let's go see what's happening on. Come on!"

Ignoring protests from the teacher, the entire class streamed outside, across the school front lawn and into the square. The children were a bit awestruck to be so close to the giant dragons which, before now, they had all seen only from high above. The students stopped at the edge of the square, keeping a safe distance between themselves and the dragons. All except Marina. She went directly through the crowd of dragons to Roan and Zelina.

"Hi Roan," Marina caressed his chocolaty head as she spoke. "What's going on?"

"We're here for the meeting that I came to tell Dad about last night," Eli answered.

As if on cue, the doors of the Zimley government building opened across the square and out stepped the town council leaders. Master Oliver in the lead, they all descended the stairs down to the mosaic tiled town square. Eli and Marina's father was there behind Oliver looking a bit overwhelmed at the sight before him. Oliver stopped a few steps beyond the stairs. Looking around he noted the crowd of citizens gathering around the edge of the square, including what now looked like all the school children.

Looking straight at Zonar, Oliver began politely enough, "Welcome Zonar and other members of the great dragon council! Welcome to our humble town square. It is most unusual for you dragons to summon us, the leaders of Zimley, to a meeting. What is the meaning of this?"

So much for polite introductions, Eli thought.

"Yes, it is unusual," Zonar's voice boomed above the crowd, making certain that all in attendance could hear him clearly. "We have a most unusual situation to bring before you."

"We're listening, though I don't know what could possibly be so unusual as to warrant your landing in the center of town. That is strictly against our agreed upon peaceful code."

"Yes, and we ask your forgiveness in that. But as you will now hear, this situation is so grave that I felt it must be discussed before all citizens of Zimley, not just behind the closed doors of your chambers with the forest-side windows open for dragons to look through, as we have always met in the past," Zonar's response was patient, though very firm.

"There is a group of humans, not all that unlike yourselves, who are in grave danger. Their people are being attacked, killed and even eaten alive by terrible beasts called the tarkoza. The dragon council leaders feel bound to go to their assistance before their people are completely destroyed."

"And who exactly are these unheard-of people?" Oliver asked in a voice dripping with suspicion.

"They are the Jolarans, the forest people from across the sea," Zonar answered. "Your brothers."

A murmur rose from the crowd gathered around the square. Even the Zimley council

members shook heads and murmured amongst themselves.

Oliver cleared his throat and called for silence. Waiting as much for effect as for silence, he held up a hand until the crowd settled down.

"Zonar, I'm surprised at you. Demanding a meeting with us, and then telling us you want to go save our enemies, the very people from whom you have agreed to protect us! How dare you!" Oliver's voice rose to a near yell.

Zonar chuckled at Oliver's lack of self control. "Relax, Master Oliver, remember your high blood pressure. Before you get angry with me, let us explain. I insist you hear what the patrol dragons have witnessed before making any decisions." Zonar's voice was deafening and as firm as a boulder while his steely eyes gazed directly into Oliver's.

Without waiting for the humans to respond, Zonar began calling his council leaders forward. One by one each dragon recounted the scenes from the forests and coast beyond the great sea. From the normally quiet coastal patrols to the growing numbers of tarkoza and their vicious attacks on the Jolaran people, to the daring and bloody rescue of Kane's family only the day before, the dragons recalled in great detail everything they had witnessed. Even little Celeste was called upon to give her account. Finally, it was Eli's turn to describe the scene he had witnessed during the rescue.

At last, Zonar asked Roan to recount for the Zimleys his amazing "find" on the water the previous morning. With a quavering voice, the little dragon told of his return flight with Zonar, spotting something floating and backtracking to identify what he had seen. Roan then reported to the Zimleys that he found someone, not something.

"Now I would like you all to meet the young man Roan found. May I present to you Kane and his mother, Anaya," Zonar introduced them with a formal bow.

Kane and Anaya stepped from behind the dragons and moved toward the town council leaders with caution.

"Jolarans! Their presence here is a violation of our peace agreement. Seize them!" ordered Oliver.

Galen instantly planted his thick, muscular front legs on either side of Kane and Anaya. His golden chest rose above them and his serpentine neck curved over them to glare at Oliver. With fire burning in his eyes, Galen spoke, "They are under my personal protection. *You* will not lay a hand on

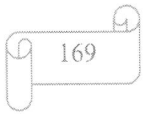

these people. You will listen to them, Oliver!"

Zonar moved closer to Oliver at the same moment. "He is right, Oliver. I insist you hear what our guests have to say. Kane acted out of brave desperation to seek aid for his people. In spite of knowing the potential consequences of death, he risked his life and that of his family to contact the dragons. Some of the purest bravery I have ever witnessed," Zonar began with vehemence in his voice that Eli had never before heard.

"We rescued Kane's mother, Anaya, and his younger brother yesterday from a deadly tarkoza attack. Without the dragon patrol, these people would now be dead. In our conversations last evening, I found Anaya to be a gentle and timid woman of great patience and resolve. She deserves to be heard here in your great square," Zonar finished and turned his head to Kane and Anaya.

Kane moved a few steps closer, bowed his head respectfully toward Oliver as he had seen Zonar do at the outset of the meeting. Straightening his shoulders, Kane addressed the Zimley council.

"Our people are being slaughtered. Before the tarkoza were awakened by the smoking mountains, we were not even certain of their existence. The tarkoza were only legends. But the legends have been proven true. We have no defense against these huge beasts. None but the hope of the dragons coming to our aid."

Anaya joined her son saying, "We live a simple life in the Jolaran forests. Each clan has their own hunting territory within the forests. Until the attacks by the tarkoza, no one ventured near the coast. This has been the way of my people for many generations. The fear of the mighty dragons patrolling our coasts ensured that we never ventured far from our homes." She looked around the council before continuing.

"Things are different now," Anaya's soft voice pleaded. "There is a danger greater than we ever dreamed could be true. If the dragons are not

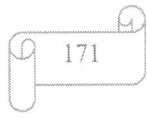

allowed to help us, I fear there will be none of our people left to carry on our way of life."

"If you allow the dragons to fight the tarkoza for us, we promise that our people will never bother you again," Kane spoke up now, sharing the plan he had formed so long ago as his family journeyed toward the coast.

Oliver's skin boiled crimson with anger. He turned and privately addressed the council. Not waiting for individual responses, Oliver turned back to the enormous group before him.

"The arrogance of this youth will not be tolerated! What the boy and his mother propose is in direct opposition to our laws governing the peace agreement. We will not consent to such action!" Oliver's voice rose as he spoke further. "We will not hear of our wonderful dragons putting themselves at risk to intervene for these savage people."

"You can't do that," Eli rushed forward to join his new friends in front of Galen. "Kane risked his life to ask for our help. He hoped that our people would show compassion and be willing to allow the dragons to protect us both. They're not savage and they do not want to threaten us in any way!"

"That's right," Marina's voice now joined the

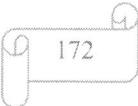

fray. "I think if our beautiful dragons are willing to help these people, then the least we can do is to let them. If I recall my history, the Zimleys would no longer be here if not for the dragons."

"This debate is *over*," Oliver cried. "Remove these people from our town square at once." Shaking in anger, he pointed a finger, at Kane and Anaya.

"Then our peace agreement is also over," Zonar bent his head down to Oliver's level and smiled a very sinister smile.

Mary Harrison

Chapter 23

Dawson Harcourt and the Brothers' Legend

Dawson Harcourt elbowed past Oliver at that same moment that Oliver demanded for Kane and Anaya's removal. His voice showed the calm control typical of the peacemaker that he was on the council.

"Kane shared with us the legend of his people about the tarkoza. Perhaps it is time for us to recall one of Zimley's oldest legends for ourselves. I suggest that all citizens, dragons and guests get

themselves comfortably seated for the telling of this treasured old legend."

A threatening glare from Zonar drove Oliver to seat himself on the lowest step at the edge of the square. Other council members followed suit. With quiet murmurs the citizens gathered around the edges of the square all found seats on benches or on the ground. The students as well, dropped to the grass in front of the school. Likewise the dragons all made themselves comfortable.

"I just love a good story," Zelina said while crossing her front paws, a twinkle shining in her eyes.

Dawson then slowly, with great care, walked to the top step in front of the government building. He turned to face the crowd. Clearing his throat, he raised his hands and began.

"Long ago, before the founding of our great town of Zimley, before there were houses, or laws or education, there lived in this lush valley a large and wonderful family. The family had many sons and daughters. These children all helped their family to live off the land. Some enjoyed growing food in gardens and even ventured into the forests to discover new foods that could be cultivated. Other children became skilled hunters who journeyed into the mountain foothills and the surrounding forests to hunt for game, always returning with enough to feed the family well for quite a long time.

"One day the two eldest sons, Zimel and Jolar, argued with each other. Zimel said it was a far better life to cultivate gardens, producing delicious crops for the family to eat. Jolar said the truest and most honorable pursuit was to hunt for wild game, providing enough meat to sustain the family through the long, cold winters.

"Well, the brothers continued to argue about whose way provided best for the family. Finally, one day their father could take no more of his sons' argument. He brought the young men together and gave them a challenge.

"I want you each to gather or grow as much food for our family as you possibly can. When winter arrives, we shall see who has stored up the most food. Then it will be determined whose way can provide best for our family in the future. You must each leave our comfortable valley during the growing and hunting season. You shall be on your own to hunt, gather and grow for this one long season. When the season changes, wherever you are, you will know that it is time to return to your family's home."

"So with their father's instructions, the two

determined brothers set off. Zimel traveled to the next valley where he planted crops and gathered food from the forest. He also built huts so he could store and preserve his crops for winter and his return to the family. Jolar, on the other hand, set off over the northern mountains, hunting for game, drying the meat and hiding it in caches along his way.

"The growing season passed with great anticipation in the valley. Everyone waited with mounting excitement to see which brother would bring back the more plentiful supply.

"At last, the first frost came upon the valley. Soon after, Zimel returned to the family home pushing a huge cart full of produce. He took some of the younger brothers and sisters, along with his father and mother, and showed them his generous storehouses, all filled with delicious grains and produce for the winter. That evening there was a joyous celebration over Zimel's success. But their father declared the contest was not complete until Jolar returned with his supply.

"Eagerly the family awaited his return, knowing the journey over the mountains would have taken him a greater time. Every evening, the family went to sleep, a little more saddened without Jolar's return.

"The winter storms soon descended upon the valley. Snows were fierce and deep that year. Still the family waited and hoped for their missing brother to return.

"By spring there was still no sign of Jolar. With a deep grief, the father declared his precious son lost to the savage conditions of the mountain forests. He announced that Zimel's way of cultivating produce and gathering from the nearby forests to be the best life for the family. Ever after, no one in the family hunted. The family only enjoyed meat from animals that they had captured, tamed and raised before the contest."

Dawson Harcourt paused and looked solemnly around the gathered crowd.

"Thus ended the legend told among our people for so long. Nothing was known about Jolar's fate for many, many generations. Not until the time of the grievous invasion when the hunters from across the sea came and took our animals and other food. Their invasion caused the horrible conflict that threatened our very existence. If not for the dragons intervening on our behalf, all of Zimley would have been overcome. The dragons drove the savage hunters back across the sea."

A silence, deep and complete settled over the crowd as Harcourt waited for the legend to sink into

the minds of everyone present.

Clearing his throat, Harcourt continued, "My friends do any of you recall the name of those invaders from across the sea? Kane just told us his people call themselves the Jolarans. It seems clear to me that Jolar was not lost as our legend tells, but that he found others, settled among the forests across the sea and raised a large and prosperous family of his own. My fellow citizens, can you not see that Kane's people are our brothers, for we all share the same ancestors?"

"Father," Marina was the first to find her voice. "Is this why it is against the law to tell the legend of Zimley?"

"Yes, my child, it is," Dawson looked tenderly at the innocence of his daughter. "After the invasion, some of our leaders knew the truth, that the savage hunters were descendants of Jolar, the lost brother. Our people were very proud of our new alliance with the dragons. To keep people who had been so frightened during the conflict from seeing the truth, the leaders banned the telling of this legend."

He paused and glared at other council members before continuing, "Fortunately, some families continued to tell their children of the family that founded our culture. I am grateful that my

grandfathers were among those brave souls who continued to share our true heritage. And I can say true heritage, for very late last night I checked the historical archives and the tales of the brothers, Zimel and Jolar, are still recorded in our ancient history."

Mary Harrison

Chapter 24

Decisions

While the council members and crowd were all still quietly contemplating this new revelation about the Zimleys' heritage, Zonar rose to his full height, stretching his neck far above the humans. Bending his neck around, Zonar addressed the crowd of citizens, ignoring the town council for the time being.

"So, now we have here before us a brave young man, a descendant of the long lost Jolar, whose family waited so long for his return. What

do the citizens of Zimley feel we should do with this young man and his mother?"

Zonar's tail twitched. He waited, surveying the crowd.

Again it was Marina's voice that spoke up first, "I think we should help them. It's like helping our own family!"

Others murmured their agreement, slowly at first, then with gathering force.

"Help them, help them!" the school children began a chant that was taken up quickly by the rest of the gathered citizens.

Zonar smiled, "Ah, my caring young friend. Your love for others pleases me a great deal. It is that love that will make you a wonderful dragon-keeper one day very soon."

Marina's eyes widened at this revelation. Zonar had just picked her to be the next apprentice dragon-keeper! But she didn't get a chance to dwell on her amazing blessing just yet, for Zonar had turned back to Master Oliver and the town council.

"And what does the ruling council say now?" Zonar questioned.

Oliver's lip twitched. Sweat formed on his brow and his chubby hands shook uncontrollably. Oliver cleared his throat.

"We must confer briefly over this decision."

Oliver tried to appear brave and self-assured as he straightened himself before Zonar. He turned and gestured for other council members to join him in a tight circle. Dawson Harcourt remained on the top step above while other council men and women gathered. Speaking in hushed voices with heads together, the council wasted no time in coming to a decision.

"We have reached a final decision in the matter of the boy and his mother," Oliver spoke in a loud and officious tone as he turned back to the crowd. "It is the considered opinion of the ruling council of Zimley that our peace treaty with the dragons remains binding. The boy, Kane, and his mother, Anaya, are in violation of the law. By their own admission they have inhabited the forbidden coast of Jolara. Crossing the sea to the Zimley coast is punishable by death, but in deference to the fondness they have generated among our people, the council will allow them to live. They will, however, be returned immediately to the lands of Jolara. Their fate beyond that is entirely up to them. Our citizens and our dragon protectors are strictly forbidden from aiding the Jolarans further. The council has spoken!"

Galen jumped to defend his precious new friends and stood squarely above the two. Anaya

gasped and nearly collapsed. Kane circled his arms protectively around his mother. Crestfallen, he could not believe what he had just heard. After all that he had risked, their situation so desperate, now they were to be coldly turned away without another thought. Kane's turmoil of thoughts was broken almost immediately by a shout.

"You can't do that! Returning them to Jolara without help is a death sentence." Fire burned in Eli's eyes as he moved to face Oliver directly, eye to eye. "Kane is my friend, and I will not see him returned back to Jolara to a certain and brutal death. I don't care if I am the only one, I will help him fight the tarkoza. To my death if need be!"

Eli's father descended the stairs without a sound. Dawson turned and stood shoulder to shoulder with his son. Speaking in a firm voice, he said, "You won't be alone, my son, for I vow to help our brothers with every last ounce of strength and knowledge that I possess."

"I stand with you also, ready to fight," Tyffan spoke up as she joined Eli and his father.

A voice from the back of the crowd shouted above the ensuing murmurs, "Help them or renounce your positions on the council!"

Everyone turned to identify the fervent speaker on the school lawn. Eli smiled when he recognized his former science teacher, Mr. Elliot, standing on a bench, clenched fist raised above his head. Eli had always known him to have strong opinions in class. He smiled now to see the depth of feeling being voiced by his former teacher.

Before Oliver or the other council members could react, the crowd began to shout with that one brave voice. "Help them or renounce your positions. Impeach the council!"

Zonar's eyes twinkled, as if this was exactly the reaction he had desired. He let the raucous cacophony go on for a few minutes before stretching his head high and roaring for silence.

Glaring down at Oliver and the remaining council members Zonar posed a new question. "It seems the town's people desire a different decision. Do you wish to reconsider or be forced out of office...today?"

"Er, ahh, well...if it is the wish of the people. I am sure I speak for the entire council - well almost the entire council," Oliver looked at Dawson and Eli for a brief moment. "The dragons may help the Jolarans, but only to satisfy the wishes of the townspeople. Once aid has been rendered to these people, our treaty must be respected and enforced once again."

"I'll tell you how our treaty will be handled

when this is finished," Zonar roared in Oliver's trembling face. "But first we have many more people who need our aid." Turning to the crowd, Zonar began to spell out his plan. He assigned tasks to all of the townspeople, including the school children. Some prepared medical supplies, others were sent to prepare food, housing would be required to treat the injured, and still others gathered long unneeded and nearly forgotten weapons. Much to her delight, Zonar asked for Marina to join the dragon colony immediately. She was assigned to care for the injuries of the warrior dragons. Marina and Eli watched with pride as their father and Mr. Elliot were the first humans selected to ride with the dragons to the shores of Jolara. In all fifteen men would help the dragons search for and protect the surviving forest dwellers, with Eli and Kane among them.

At last, Zonar called to the all dragons present, "Make ready all of our strongest and fiercest warriors. We have no time to loose!"

With that, glimmering wings unfurled and the dragons rose as one in an elegant array of brilliant colors, creating a thunderous, powerful wind that swept over the town square.

Chapter 25

The Battle Begins

Zimzor's twin suns were at their zenith, high overhead as the dragon council returned to the colony. Eli, Tyffan, Kane and Anaya returned with the dragons in flight. Soon a procession consisting of the other men selected to join the dragon warriors, Marina, the newest apprentice keeper, and the first of the supply wagons approached the colony. Clarice Harcourt was among those selected to help care for survivors, and she, too, came in the procession. Preparations were quickly completed.

Riders were fitted with saddles; supply packs and weapons handed out, and battle instructions given by Zonar.

Fifteen powerful dragons would carry the men in search of surviving Jolarans in the forests. Any that could be plucked from the forest would be swept away to safety on the coast. Using Kane's family cave as a base, survivors would be cared for there by Tyffan, Anaya and Clarice. Jorno, Tremor, Sylvie and Rosamae would remain on the beach to protect this group. Zelina, too, would work at the survivor's cave, determining if any of the injured Jolarans required greater medical care than the small group could offer. If so, she would then assign them to one of the smaller dragons for transport to the Zimley coast. Roan and Celeste would act as messengers between the beach and the warriors over the forests. Zonar would lead the remaining warriors in battle against any and all tarkoza to be found in the forests.

So with very little time wasted, the massive group gathered on the beach beneath the dragon caves, ready for battle. A slight nod from Zonar was all the order necessary for the mass to rise into the sky. A host of scales glimmered in the sun as the sky became a sea of dazzling colors. The crowd of Zimleys remaining on the beach watched the sight in awe, barely noticing the wind from all those churning wings that blew their hair.

Devon and Marina were among those in the watching crowd. The pair had been assigned to assist medical workers on the Zimley coast caring for injured dragons. Both waved in excited, yet nervous anticipation of the events to come. Together they watched until the last dragon was out of sight. Turning back up the path, Devon set about his first task, that of familiarizing Marina with the layout of caves inside the dragon colony.

~ ~ ~

As the coast slipped away behind them, Eli gripped his saddle while his stomach churned. He felt his heart had moved to his throat. Gazing ahead, he remembered his first visit to the coast of Jolara and the horrific scene his group had found there. He looked over toward Galen, where Kane also strained to see ahead, concern wearing heavy upon his face. Eli caught Kane's eye and held out his fist, then crossed it over and tapped his own chest - the Jolaran sign of companionship that Kane had shown him. Kane's worry lines eased a bit as he returned the signal to Eli.

It seemed like no time before Eli heard Handrill's voice above the wind.

"The coast comes into view," his deep voice

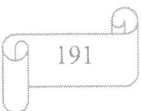

cried.

Eli leaned around Handrill's thick neck. Sure enough their goal was in sight. Looking around, Eli could see the other Zimley men also straining to get a first glimpse of the Jolaran coast, so filled with danger.

Before long the massive group set down on the beach beneath the cave where Kane, Anaya and Devon had sought refuge. Tremor, Rosamae and Jorno, a huge and ancient, green dragon, moved toward the cave entrance and waited while their riders climbed down. Anaya, Tyffan and Clarice immediately began climbing up to the cave, carrying their heavy supply packs with them. Sylvie waited patiently while the supply packs she carried were unloaded and passed up to the cave. The four dragons set up a protective perimeter while the women began the task of preparing the cave for wounded. Zelina quickly organized the smaller and younger dragons to assist with protecting the perimeter until they were needed as messengers or to carry the wounded across the sea.

Once Zonar was confident that the group on the beach was prepared, he looked over his massive group of warriors and he cleared his throat before giving final instructions.

"The time has come. Work together in groups

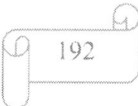

of three or four attacking from all sides of each tarkoza. Remember, their claws are longer than ours and sharp. Watch out for fangs. If any of you are struck, return to the beach at once. I want no losses among you - my friends. " Zonar dispatched fifteen warriors and riders to search the forest for survivors. Looking at his remaining warriors, Zonar tipped his head in a respectful salute to them all and said, "The battle begins!"

~ ~ ~

Zonar led his group, consisting of the oldest and largest dragons over the central region of forest, following the river upstream. In almost no time, the group heard the piercing roar an attacking tarkoza, followed by terrified human screams. Diving into the forest fray, Zonar dug his claws deep into the thick fur and muscles on the tarkoza's shoulders. He was followed in an instant by a sickening blow from the tail of Dentax and claws to the head administered by Calistor. The tarkoza howled in pain and protest. It lashed at the sky in its attempts to bring down the attacking dragons. Zonar and his companions were not to be out matched. They continued their attack in swift rounds, dealing blow after blow to the massive tarkoza, claws and teeth ripping into flesh. At last the huge beast crumbled to the ground, gave up one final, feeble scream and then lay still.

Zonar and the others circled above, breathing heavily, as they waited for a rescue team to arrive and scoop up the stunned, but safe, Jolarans below.

Chapter 26

Survivors

Eli, still aboard the elder dragon, Handrill, followed by Kane secure on Galen's strong shoulders, and Dawson, carried by the muscular giant of a dragon, Chesmare, all headed above the southern forest together as Zonar had dispatched each group from the beach. The three human riders leaned out and down, straining for the best view between the trees below. Pointing to his left, Eli signaled the others of his sighting. Below, three beleaguered Jolarans cowered inside a flimsy

shelter, the oldest peeking out, eyes nervously surveying the area for danger. The dragon group descended without hesitation. Kane explained as quickly as possible that the previously dreaded, legendary dragons had arrived to help. The trio of survivors, trembling from the shock of dragons landing in front of them on top of their harrowing experiences outrunning the tarkoza, meekly followed Eli's instructions as he made haste to fasten them into spare saddles aboard each of the dragons.

The group returned to the beach without wasting any time, for every minute was precious in the race against the tarkoza. After depositing the first survivors, Eli, Kane and Dawson climbed back aboard their dragons and again set off over the forest.

With each successive trip, every rescue team brought back more frightened and injured Jolarans and deposited them into the care of Tyffan's team on the beach. Soon, the group was overwhelmed by the number of injured. In her orderly fashion, Zelina began to assign young dragons to carry medical slings with the most severely wounded back to the Zimley coast and the waiting teams of doctors. She sent orders with them to return with a volunteer corps of doctors and nurses willing to care for survivors in the rugged conditions of the beach and cave. Tyffan, Anaya and Clarice wasted no time in alerting Zelina to those survivors needing more medical care than they could provide.

Comforting the remaining frightened survivors was nearly as great a task as the rescue itself. In what seemed to many of the survivors as only an instant, the Jolarans found themselves cowering on the forbidden coast surrounded by dragons and the victorious Zimley people of the ancient legends. Anaya proved to be gifted at comforting and guiding her people. With gentleness, she seated the trembling survivors, offered food, water and blankets, all the while telling and retelling her own family's story of survival on the coast and Kane's daring efforts to seek help from the dragons.

~ ~ ~

Further north above the forest, Kane signaled the others. Below a blood thirsty tarkoza feasted on human flesh. Not far away, Kane spotted a young boy clinging high in the branches of a leafless oak tree, certain to be the tarkoza's next meal without speedy intervention.

Handrill, Galen and Chesmare circled above. Quickly it was decided, with only a few nods, that Kane and Galen would rescue the boy while the

others disposed of the tarkoza. Eli and his father each reached into the pack behind them, pulled out a heavy, short-hafted, multi-pointed spear and braced for the battle that was about to take place.

Handrill attacked first, clawing the tarkoza on the back of the neck while it ate. Eli leaned down and plunged his spear into its back. They were followed by a terrifying roar as Chesmare swooped down, claws and teeth ripping into the beast's back. Dawson used his spear more like a club, leveling several blows to the head.

The angry tarkoza rose on its hind legs to its full height of nearly twenty feet. Snarls vibrated from deep in the animal's throat as it lashed out with huge paws. One swipe glanced off of Chesmare's heavy tail. Chesmare circled back without seeming to notice and delivered a heavy thud from that same tail across the tarkoza's forehead.

Handrill and Chesmare continued to dive in from different angles, keeping the furious beast off balance. Before long, Handrill saw the opening he needed. He lunged forward, grabbed the neck of the tarkoza in his mighty jaws, lifted the beast and shook hard. When Handrill finally let go, the tarkoza fell limp against the rocks below.

While all of this was taking place, Kane and

Galen soared toward the terrified boy in the tree. Upon seeing the huge golden dragon, the boy swayed and lost his grip. Branches broke as Galen forced himself closer. Kane leaned out dangerously far and attempted to scoop the teetering boy into his arms. But the terrified boy drew himself tightly against the trunk of the great oak tree.

"I can't get in that close," Galen called to Kane. "My size is too great. I could topple this old tree trying to reach the lad."

Kane wrinkled his forehead in frustration. "We need one of the smaller dragons to reach him."

Almost as if on cue Roan flew toward the group.

"I have a message for you," the small dragon shouted as he arrived. "There is a group of survivors to the north in a clearing beside some huge fir trees. You are the closest rescue group."

"Okay, Roan, we'll get them, but first we need your help," Eli answered as he pointed Roan toward Galen, Kane and the huge oak tree.

Roan needed no further instruction. He quickly spotted the terrified little boy clinging to the inner trunk high above the ground. With all the grace of a seasoned flier, Roan nimbly darted between branches above the boy, reached down with his front claws and plucked the surprised

youngster from his perch. Roan heard Kane's call and flew the boy to him. Kane reached out and received the boy from Roan's firm grasp. As he drew the shaking boy close and seated the child

between himself and Galen's neck, Kane gazed into familiar eyes.

"Maxell?" Kane asked.

The boy could only nod in affirmation.

"Where is your family?"

"Gone. Eaten. They've all been eaten," came Maxell's quavering response as he gave in to tears.

"You know this child?" Galen inquired of Kane as he rose above the forest trees and turned toward the coast.

"Yes! His father, Nantell, drove my family from our hunting grounds just before the first tarkoza attack. I was so angry at him for sending us away, but now it looks like Nantell saved our lives."

Kane encircled little Maxell in his arms and gently rocked the crying boy as he considered this turn of events while Galen silently winged his way back to the rescue cave.

~ ~ ~

"Mother, I've found someone who really needs you," Kane called as he approached carrying a small sobbing boy.

"There now, you're safe, everything will get better. You'll see," Anaya wasted no time in offering words of comfort as she lifted the boy from Kane's arms. Looking into his tear stained face, Anaya's eye widened with recognition.

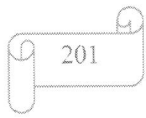

"You're Nantell's youngest son!" amazement and concern filled her voice. "Where are your mother and father?"

Maxell crumbled into deeper sobs as he clung to Anaya.

"He's all that's left," Kane answered.

"Maxell, dear, you are not alone," Anaya comforted. "We're your family now. Things will get better. See, we have the dragons to help us."

Maxell seemed to melt into her shoulders as Anaya continued to sooth him. He ventured a peek over his new mother's shoulder at Kane and the enormous golden dragon that had flown him to safety. The boy held his breath as he watched the pair rise up and over the forest again, searching for more survivors.

Chapter 27

Coming Together

Days past, filled with vicious battles. Many survivors were plucked from the forest, some only moments before being attacked by tarkoza. One the beach and in the cave used as their base, Zelina, Anaya, Tyffan and Clarice worked without ceasing to aid the survivors and direct the necessary medical care. Zelina, an elder dragon of many years and extensive wisdom, needed little rest to work at peak performance. The humans, however, were nearing exhaustion when Zelina stepped in with a

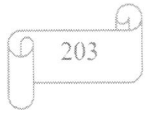

plan.

"You ladies are going to wear yourselves out if you keep up this pace. We need more help on this side of the sea. I can't see sending more than the most seriously wounded over to the Zimley side for treatment. But, I think you three could use a break." She turned to one of the young dragons from Eli's training group.

"Verde, I want to fly over to our colony and deliver a message to Razine for me. Have her select workers from Zimley to help us on this coast. Many of the survivors are children and we need some capable child care workers. Ask her to pick some other volunteers to help comfort, and care for the Jolaran people. More cooks are needed. We also need more supplies – food and blankets for the survivors."

Verde nodded her understanding and took off into the wind, across the sea to the east.

~ ~ ~

Hearing the news and Zelina's request, Razine, a fleet dragon in her prime, wasted no time. She sent fleet-footed messengers into town to Miss Hawkins, the school principal once feared by Eli, who had taken charge of organizing volunteers and workers at Zonar's request. Miss Hawkins immediately called for half of the childcare workers from the town's daycare centers and nurseries to be sent across the sea. Many parents, mothers and fathers alike, also volunteered for the task. Word was sent for merchants to offer more blankets, pillows, cots and other supplies for the relief effort.

Miss Hawkins then turned her attention to the food issue. She understood that the workers on the beach had only minimal equipment for cooking at their disposal. Being the practical person that she was, she felt no need to complicate their situation by sending only cooking supplies, so she marched directly to the largest bakery in town.

"Good morning, Hans. I need your help." Miss Hawkins wasted no time getting to the point of her need and plan. "The survivors on the Jolaran beach are in desperate need more food supplies. I want you to organize all the bakers and cooking establishments in town. We must send food prepared and ready to serve to the survivors. Nothing too fancy, but it must be nutritious and easy to serve to frightened people. Can you handle that?"

Hans, a jolly, tall man who was well liked by all his customers, smiled broadly from behind his counter. "Of course I can. You just send me dragons to carry the baked goods across the sea. I will make sure that all the baking and dining

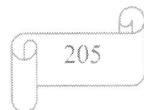

establishments in town turn out a bounty of
delicious food to meet the needs of our Jolaran
brothers and sisters. You may take the first load
from my own bakery right now."

Miss Hawkins watched with respect and
pride as her fellow Zimleys rose to the somewhat
overwhelming task of meeting the basic needs of the
Jolarans. In less than half an hour Verde and
several other young dragons were loaded with
packs filled with fresh fruits and vegetables that
could be eaten raw, others carried foods that were
cooked and packed into individual serving
containers. Still more packs contained breads and
rolls baked only that morning. Blankets, pillows
and more medical supplies completed the load. A
number of the smaller adult dragons had already
begun shuttling volunteer childcare workers across
the sea.

~ ~ ~

Back on the Jolaran side of the sea, Clarice
watched with relief as young dragons began
arriving with workers and supplies. She and Anaya
wasted no time in organizing them into groups to
care for children, wounded or newly arrived
survivors. Tyffan and several other teens that had
just arrived removed packs of food and supplies
from the dragons as soon as they landed. Tyffan

directed the distribution of food, first to the survivors who had most recently arrived.

An exhausted Anaya sat down on a boulder at the base of the cliff and observed the scene before her. The Zimley workers who had just arrived immediately set about meeting the needs of her people. No task appeared to be either beneath the Zimleys, or too difficult. Her former enemies reached out with loving care to the Jolaran people. As she pondered this incredible sight, a Zimley woman approached her.

"Anaya, my name is Marie. I saw you face the council in our town square. You're very brave and I admire your courage, but you look exhausted.

Let me help here, so you can get some rest."

Gazing up at Marie through dumbstruck eyes, Anaya shook her head before she was able to reply. "You're supposed to be my enemy, Marie, yet here you are, risking you life just by being on this beach and you want to help my people. Why? What's happening here?"

"Without the laws that have kept our peoples apart for many generations, I think we may just find ourselves to be more alike than different, just as Zonar said," Marie chuckled as she reached to help Anaya up. "Now, my dear, you need some rest. Is that cave where you and your boys lived?"

Anaya nodded in assent. Marie gently guided her up to the cave and only left after Anaya was snuggled down within her own sleeping furs at the back of the cave.

A still timid Maxell followed in silence and peered in from the cave entrance. After Marie tiptoed out of the cave so as not to disturb Anaya, Maxell slipped back into the recess of the cave. The little boy was so grief stricken from the tragic loss of his family that he feared being apart from his new mother for more than just a few moments. As Anaya drifted off to sleep, Maxell crept over, lifted the edge of the fur and crawled in beside her. Anaya wrapped her arms around her new son and murmured in his ear. Maxell felt cozy and safe for the first time in weeks. He snuggled close, grateful for the security and comfort he received from Anaya. He, too, soon fell asleep, blissfully free from the ravages of these past months.

Mary Harrison

Chapter 28

Trapped

It was late afternoon and the day had been particularly hot and humid, especially deep within the forest where trees hung with moss and moisture dripped from water laden leaves and branches. The morning mist had never lifted from this part of the forest, making the suns' rays streak through in streams of bluish haze. Eli and Kane aboard their dragon friends continued to work together to rescue Jolarans from the approaching jaws of tarkoza. Many were the last survivors of formerly large

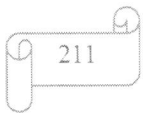

families.

Kane saw him first; young hunter on the forest floor trying in desperation to free someone from beneath the overhanging moss and vines. The hunter was just a boy of about twelve. Under usual circumstances, his being alone in the forest would be quite acceptable, even normal. Boys his age often ventured off on their own hunting forays. Jolaran fathers considered this good training for every young hunter. But these were not normal circumstances. The danger of being alone was far too great for this young boy. Kane knew they had to intervene and help before the boy and his unseen companion were found by a tarkoza.

"Galen, we need to get down to him. How close can you land?"

Surveying the area, Galen shook his head. "Not close enough. The trees here are too dense for a dragon my size to land."

"How about that clearing to the north?" Eli interjected as he and Jorno circled above.

"I don't like it," Jorno shook his head as he scanned the area. "It's too far. You and Kane will have to travel back to through the thickest part of the undergrowth. The canopy is so dense it is nearly impenetrable for Galen and me should you need our aid. No, I don't like that idea one little bit."

"I don't see any other alternative," Galen reasoned as he continued to scan the area for a better option. "If we don't get our riders down to collect him, this lad will be a snack for the next tarkoza that happens along."

It was decided. Eli and Kane would make haste through the undergrowth and seek out the lone boy. Kane would return to Galen with the boy, while Eli would free his companion and then bring him back as well. Jorno would circle overhead as a lookout while the boys were in dangerous positions on the ground.

Both dragons made one further circle above, eyes straining to pierce the mist as they probed the forest for any approaching tarkoza. Jorno conceded that the area appeared safe enough for a brief rescue on foot. The dragons set down in the small clearing about one hundred yards from the young hunter.

Kane and Eli ran, jumped and nimbly climbed over fallen trees making their way toward the boy.

"You there, we saw you from above and we're here to help," Kane called ahead, not wanting to frighten the boy. "Who's that you're trying to free?"

Eli and Kane slowed their approach; the struggling boy's back was toward them.

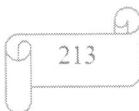

"It's not who....uhhh," The boy strained to pull a log free from the tangled vines. "It's a what."

Eli and Kane ducked beneath the hanging moss and vines and found themselves looking at a magnificent creature, the elusive and shy moss horse of the forests. Dark green fur bunched up in clumps looking very much like moss. The horse's mane glowed a beautiful neon shade of lime green and flashed every time the animal struggled.

"It's bioluminescent!" Eli gasped. "I've only read about creatures like these. They once inhabited the mountains north of Zimley. Most people believe they are now extinct, but I guess they're not." He then looked at the boy who continued to struggle in his attempts to free the moss horse. "I'm Eli and this is Kane. We're here to get you to safety. There are still many tarkoza roaming this part of the forest."

"I'm Tanner and I'm not leaving him to be the next meal of beast food. Help me get him loose. Please!"

The stately creature was wedged between three fallen trees and caught in a net of vines. Every time it kicked, the bone claws on its foreleg joints became more tangled in the vines. Realizing they had no time to argue and convince Tanner to come along and leave the trapped animal, Kane and Eli

exchanged a quick glance, and then each pulled out a hunting knife and went to work on the vines. Progress seemed painfully slow to Kane as the three boys hacked away at the vines. Eli slid between one of the logs and the moss horse. Knowing he was in a dangerous position, his head all too near the protruding bone claws, Eli spoke to the horse in a gentle, soothing voice. Reaching out, he took one foreleg in his hand and with the other began to separate the troublesome vines. Kane saw that Eli was making significant progress and climbed over a fallen log on the other side of the animal. He began to free the right foreleg, although he resorted to cutting the vines off the bone claws, taking care not to cut into the horse's leg.

"Now we're getting somewhere," Eli began. Looking over at Kane, his face suddenly drained of all color and he froze in place.

"What's wrong Eli?" Kane already guessed at the cause of Eli's sudden change.

"We're being stalked," Eli whispered as he freed the left leg completely. "Tanner, get under this horse with us, now!"

Kane reached out and grabbed Tanner's arm, pulling him down, head first over the log.

"What do we do now?" Tanner's voice barely audible. He shook uncontrollably between Kane and Eli.

"Keep still and quiet," Eli instructed.

"That thing already sees the horse," Kane whispered back. "It probably also smells us by now, too. If it kills the moss horse, we're next! We need help from the dragons right now."

Together Eli and Kane began to shout for Galen and Jorno, just as Jorno spotted a blue shape moving in the forest below. He roared for Galen and proceeded to crash downward through the forest canopy, breaking branches and toppling trees as he flew. Galen was instantly airborne and over the location in moments. He, too, dove down causing a tremendous and thundering racket as he broke even more ancient trees on his descent.

The tarkoza was temporarily distracted from its prey; moss horse and boys alike. It reared up to battle the approaching dragons, only to knock over two more young trees as if they were tiny blocks.

Galen and Jorno fought a difficult battle against this particular beast. It seemed more clever and to have sharper reflexes than most other tarkoza. Its size was also among the largest seen so far. The two dragons concentrated on their battle, unable to switch their focus to the boys for even a second. Trees continued to crash around the trio and the battle raged. The tarkoza jumped at Galen just as Jorno flung his tail at its head. Jorno missed the head and only landed a sound thud along the side of its chest, angering the tarkoza further.

Responding to the sounds of battle reverberating throughout the forest, other dragons and riders soon joined the fray. Dentax plummeted down to sink his claws into the back of the tarkoza, pulling it down in time to prevent Galen from receiving a paw full of glistening green claws to his underbelly. Zonar responded by grabbing the outstretched paw in his jaws and shook hard, breaking the foreleg of the creature. Dawson, aboard Chesmare, thrust his spear into the creature's back. Jorno and Sylvie finished it off with bites and claws to the head and belly.

Landing atop the devastation, Galen and Jorno looked around in frantic attempts to locate Eli and Kane.

"Eli, where are you?" Jorno roared.

"We're trapped under the trees."

The dragons jumped off the pile in shock, not willing to risk crushing the boys by adding their weight to the mountain of trees covering their young friends.

"Help, we can't get out," an unfamiliar voice called in desperation.

The dragons and riders listened to the faint

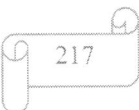

cries from somewhere beneath the pile of wreckage. Dawson was the first to identify the exact location of their calls for help. He signaled for quiet and listened again, then called to his son.

"Eli, are either of you injured?"

"I'm not, but Kane is bleeding. He was hit in the side of the head. And there are four of us trapped under here. It's pretty tight and we can't budge these trees. There is no way for us to crawl out between them either."

"Do not worry, Eli. We will get you out," Zonar assured him.

Under Zonar's direction, the dragons began to remove the mass of toppled trees with considerable care. Many trees, now bereft of branches, could be lifted by the dragons; others were pulled or dragged off the pile. Since the surrounding area was as dense as this area had been before the battle, the dragons could not land without risking further destruction. Zonar resorted to a hasty plan of working in rotations. Two dragons at a time moved trees from the pile and deposited them in the meadow clearing where Galen and Jorno had originally landed. The next pair of dragons patrolled from above while the final two scanned the forest floor in the nearby clearings for any approaching tarkoza. The six massive warriors worked in rapid rotation, all fearing the worst would be found beneath the mound.

Gradually, the mountain of crushed, shattered and broken trees began to diminish under the steady and swift work of the dragons. The sight that was uncovered amazed Dawson and dragons alike. Beneath the greatest mass of timber, a dozen or so trees had fallen together, creating a conical shelter, each wedged against the others for mutual support. Enough space had been cleared around this pile for Zonar and Galen to land. Together with Dawson, the pair inspected the fallen teepee of trees.

"This structure has saved our riders and the boy we came to rescue," Galen observed.

"True, and a miraculous and well placed pile it is. But it appears that if we remove any one of these trees alone, the others may over balance and fall in on the boys," Zonar spoke with concern for the safety of his two most treasured riders during the many battles that had taken place within the Jolaran forests.

Dawson walked around the formation, observing it from all angles, then he called to Eli, "Son, what can you tell me about the formation of trees above you from the inside?"

Eli poked his head from under the moss

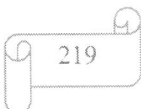

horse's belly and peered above him. "Well Dad, the first two trees that fell on us crashed into each other, sort of forming a bridge above us. I can see the broken ends of those two trees. They're balanced against each other. The other trees have all fallen against those two."

"And what is there below that shelters you and Kane?" Zonar inquired.

"We're between a triangle of fallen trees – old ones. There's a mass of vines covering us that had been hanging from the trees before everything crashed down on us. I guess you could save that we have a bit of a tree cave covered by a dense net of vines."

"OK, Eli. I see what you are describing. Give us a few minutes. I think I can figure a way to get these off without burying you any further. It may be a bit tricky, though." Turning to Zonar and Galen, Dawson explained, "If two dragons work on opposite sides of this structure you could remove approximately equal mass from each side simultaneously. That should prevent a cave in. We may need Jorno down here to steady the cone as more trees are removed."

"Excellent plan," Zonar agreed. After calling Jorno down from the sky patrol, Zonar and Galen positioned themselves on opposite sides. Each dragon grasped the outer most tree on his side and lifted. The tree structure groaned as the strain of weight sifted to the many remaining trees in the cone. As Zonar and Galen flew to the meadow to deposit their loads, Chesmare and Sylvie were quick to replace them. Just before they began to lift the next two trees off the pile a different groan emanated from below. Jorno instinctively tightened his grip on the cone of logs while Dawson moved in and listened.

"Eli, what's going on down there? Is everyone all right?"

"That was Kane groaning, Dad. His head injury may be more serious than I first thought. He's definitely in pain and not very responsive to me right now. I think you'd better hurry and get this stuff off us."

"We're working on it, son, but speed is not going to help. We don't want to make things worse by being careless or moving too fast. Try to keep Kane comfortable and quiet."

"Sure thing, Dad."

At Dawson's nod, Chesmare and Sylvie hoisted two gigantic logs from the pile. Again the structure shifted and groaned, but Jorno held the mass steady. Dentax soared down to join Zonar while Galen patrolled overhead for a short time.

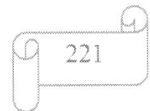

The next pair of logs was removed without further shifting from the pile. Working at a steady pace, the dragons under Dawson's skilled eye cleared away all the trees but the final two.

"OK, Zonar and Dentax need to grab hold and lift when Jorno releases these last two," Dawson looked from one dragon to the next. "Now!"

The final two logs rose with the dragons, the last of the trap removed and none had fallen in on the three trapped boys. Dawson gaped at what remained – a tangled mass of vines, so dense that the boys were not yet visible to their rescuers.

"Eli, can you see us?" Dawson called.

Eli again edged himself from beneath the moss horse as much as possible and peeked out. He smiled.

"I sure can, Dad, and boy do you look good!" Eli started to push on the vines, causing the pile to wiggle up and down.

Jorno smiled and his eyes gleamed as he saw the heap undulating. He swooped down and snatched up huge clawfuls of vines. The mass rose with him, draping down for many feet as he lifted into the sky. Dawson moved in, pushing vines aside. His joy at seeing the mass removed was replaced by amazement when the first living being he beheld was not his son, but the presumably

extinct moss horse.

"Eli, where are you?"

Eli stretched up from the opposite side of the horse to smile at his dad.

"Pretty amazing, isn't it," Eli asked as he looked at his stunned father.

"I had no idea these horses really existed."

Just then, Zonar and Dentax returned to the newly cleared area. Zonar smiled and bent his neck down to gaze into the moss horse's face.

"My, my. I haven't seen one of your kind in centuries. So this is where you've been hiding." Looking at the still amazed Dawson, Zonar explained, "These moss horses inhabited our side of the sea many years ago. We thought they had all died out in the great invasion, but it seems we were wrong." Then, turning to Eli, Zonar questioned, "Eli, I was under the impression that you and Kane were rescuing a boy when the tarkoza approached. What's this moss horse doing here?"

"We came for a boy," replied Eli, pulling Tanner from beneath the moss horse. "This is Tanner. He was trying to free someone, but from the air we couldn't tell who it was. It turned out to be this beautiful moss horse, tangled in fallen vines. We just about had him free when the tarkoza came."

"And where is Kane," Galen asked as he landed, unable to contain his concern any longer.

Again, Eli bent behind the moss horse, this time helping a very weak Kane to his feet. Dawson crossed around the young horse and helped steady

Kane, lifting him over the log. He could see that Eli had applied salve and bandages to Kane's bloodied head wound. Dawson guided Kane over to Galen and, together with Eli, helped him aboard. Eli secured Kane's safety straps as Kane bent forward, resting his head on Galen's golden neck, just below a spine.

Tanner, fearing the group would leave the moss horse behind that he had worked so desperately to save, spoke for the first time.

"What about him?" His young voice quavered as he gestured to the animal.

"Do not worry, lad. We will not leave this lovely animal hear to be eaten by the next tarkoza that passes by." Zonar assured him. Looking around the group, Zonar expressed his concern. "We have been on the ground much too long in this part of the forest. We must leave at once. Eli, is Kane secure?"

"Yes, Zonar. I've put an extra strap around him, so he'll be safe getting back."

"Good, now please secure young Tanner here on Dentax. He has a rescue saddle." Seeing Tanner's eyes widen in fear, Zonar was quick to reassure the boy. "We dragons have come to the aid of your people. We have rescued many survivors and they are all living on the coast under our protection. We're going to take you there now."

"Not without my moss horse," Tanner protested.

Dawson brought over a vine he had been working on and slipped a homemade lead over the animal's head. "Don't worry, Tanner. We won't leave him. Now, help me coax him over these logs."

Without the mass of vines entangling his legs, the moss horse stepped gracefully over the fallen logs and into the clearing, its mane sparkling as it shook its head. With Tanner on one side stroking its neck and Dawson leading while speaking softly, the horse followed as if it had always been tamed. Dawson looked up at Zonar.

"Any ideas how we get him out of here without walking?"

"Bring the animal to me." Zonar reached out his massive front legs, gracefully slipped them around the horse's middle, much like a child would carry a puppy and pulled the startled horse to his chest. The tiny horse next to Zonar's mass was no match. Dawson stroked and spoke to calm it and soon the horse hung calmly in Zonar's grip. Dawson turned to Tanner and led him over to Dentax. With Eli's help, Tanner was guided up Dentax's massive foreleg and secured in the saddle.

Zonar, Dentax and Galen leaped into the sky

so Jorno and Chesmare could land and pick up their riders. Sylvie had continued to circle overhead, eyes scanning for the ever present threat of tarkoza. Eli and Dawson wasted no time in getting seated, ready for the ride back to the beach. Then the three remaining dragons winged over the forest after their comrades.

~ ~ ~

The survivors on the beach created quite a buzz when they saw the six approaching warriors. Zonar landed first with a lovely, though very windblown moss horse in his arms. Kane hung limply from his saddle straps as Galen landed, taking care not to jar his injured rider. Dentax set down with yet another rescued child of the forest.

Tyffan and Marie ran to Kane's aid. The young women unstrapped him and lowered his limp body down Kane's foreleg. Anaya and a Clarice ran to meet them, followed by a Zimley doctor carrying a stretcher. Fear gripped Anaya and tears ran unchecked down her face. She stooped beside Kane as the doctor began his examination.

"His pupils are responsive and he's lost quite a bit of blood. But I think we're just looking at a concussion, not a skull fracture here." Doctor Kline looked up at Anaya. "Let's get him on a sling and

over to the Zimley shore where we can make certain."

Tyffan and Marie helped Dr. Kline position Kane on the stretcher. Zelina had observed the fallen warrior and selected a young adult dragon, Meerade, who was adept at carrying the medical slings. Zelina also came with a saddle for Anaya. Concern and confusion swept across Anaya's face. In an instant Clarice was by her side.

"You belong with Kane right now, Anaya. Don't worry, Marie and I will take care of Maxell and the others for you," Clarice spoke in a gentle voice as she guided Anaya to the waiting Meerade.

In a very short time Anaya and Kane were rising above the beach with Meerade. It was then that all eyes turned to Zonar and the prize he carried. A group of onlookers formed a wide circle around the dragon lord and the small horse he carried.

"He caught a forest horse!" young Maxell pointed as he exclaimed.

"He didn't catch it, I rescued it from the beasts," Tanner called down as he struggled to release himself from the unfamiliar straps on his saddle.

"Be still, young one and wait for Eli to release you. It will only take a moment," Dentax curled his

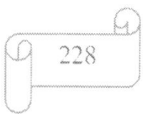

neck around to the struggling Tanner. He chose not to comment on who had actually done the rescuing.

Just then, Eli and the others also touched down on the beach. Eli sprang from Jorno's back and hurried over to Dentax. He had Tanner freed and down in mere moments. Tanner headed toward Zonar and the moss horse, giving himself a wide berth around the immense dragon. Dawson, too, was on the ground and heading toward the frightened horse. He wanted to help calm the animal before it lashed out in fear at the survivors on the beach with its deadly looking bone claws. Only after Dawson had a firm grip on the lead vine did Zonar release his hold on the moss horse.

There were whispered "oohs" and "aahs" from the crowd as Dawson and Tanner lead the horse away from the dragons. Dawson motioned a nearby doctor over to examine the horse for injury. The skilled hands of the Zimley doctor found no obvious or threatening wounds on the moss horse, but many cuts and abrasions from its misshape in the vines and trees. Mr. Elliott, Eli's former science teacher could not keep himself away from the beautiful animal which he had always taught as an extinct species of Zimzor's wildlife.

"Amazing! Simply amazing," was all Elliott could say at first. His reverie was broken by the sounds of many children asking who got to keep the wonderful, glowing horse from the forest.

"What's going to happen to it?" Maxell asked, a bit too overcome to venture getting close enough to pet the horse.

"Well, I'd say the first thing we need to do is make an enclosure to keep this moss horse safe," Elliott began. He and Dawson set about organizing the enthralled children to collect large pieces of drift wood and rocks from the beach. While Dawson and Tanner kept the horse still, Elliot and the children built a make-shift corral around them. Through all the frenzied activity surrounding it, the moss horse stood perfectly still while observing with wide brown eyes all the comings and goings.

So it happened that the ever growing colony of survivors welcomed yet another survivor into their midst.

Chapter 29

Casualties

The battles with tarkoza, both large and small, continued for many days as the dragons continued their search for the beasts. Kane's head wound healed quickly and he was back within a week's time. Many of the dragons traded off carrying riders on the search for survivors and fighting in battles. Eli, Kane and Dawson continued along with the other rescuers to tirelessly search the forests for surviving Jolaran families. Zonar and his warriors proved to be a deadly match for the tarkoza. Roan, Celeste and the other young dragons not only served as messengers but soon began to help in the search and rescue efforts.

Zonar, Handrill, Dentax and Calistor surrounded a particularly large tarkoza. Its ravenous appetite had not been satisfied by the young hunter it had recently devoured. When the dragons spotted the beast it was moving toward a terrified little girl huddled behind a rock. The child had just witnessed the death of her brother, a once strong hunter, and was frozen by fear in her hiding place.

Wasting no time, the dragon foursome swooped down and attacked. They methodically charged the tarkoza first from the rear, then sides, then above the head, always keeping the angry beast off balance. Suddenly the tarkoza reared up on hind legs to a towering twenty-three feet tall. Slashing its long claws with vengeance, the tarkoza tore into the side and haunches of Handrill.

The great old dragon was brought down by the blow. Before the tarkoza could turn its attention to the wounded dragon, Zonar flew between Handrill and his assailant, using his own body as a protective shield. Slashing claws ripped into Zonar's chest. Zonar seemed unaware of his own wounds as many of his beautiful scales fell to the ground below. He whirled around and caught the tarkoza in the head with a mighty blow from his tail.

Meanwhile Dentax and Calistor attacked in unison. Together these two knocked the tarkoza backwards exposing its unprotected belly. Calistor lunged with claws and teeth ripping into the abdomen of the vicious beast. Dentax dove for the head. Grabbing the tarkoza by the throat, he clamped down hard. Although the beast fought and squirmed to free itself from the grip of the dragons, it was to no avail. Zonar quickly joined his companions, gouging at the base of the tarkoza's head, and soon the beast breathed its last.

The frightened little girl was not forgotten during the terrifying battle; for Roan had been flying nearby and heard Zonar's shout to save the child. Bravely, Roan had darted in behind the warriors and headed straight for the rock where she cowered. Clutching the girl in his front claws, Roan began his ascent, trying to rise above the forest while keeping a safe distance from the raging battle in the clearing below.

And then it happened. A young tarkoza spotted Roan and the girl from its perch on the cliff above the clearing where the battle was being waged. Although this tarkoza was much smaller

even than Roan, it still possessed terrible claws and fangs. It also proved to have all the instincts and skill of the hunter it was born to be. Without warning, the animal reached out and slashed Roan,

ripping a huge tear, shredding the membrane of his right wing. The young beast lost its balance on the cliff and plunged over the edge as a result of its blow to Roan. It landed with a resounding thud on the very rock where the girl had hidden, ending its own life.

Poor Roan was knocked completely off balance. With his wing membrane flapping aimlessly, unable to catch the breeze, Roan could not maintain any lift on his right side. He held his grip on the girl but tumbled downward, desperately struggling to regain control. Roan flapped his wings in rapid succession and did his best using his unharmed left wing to angle their descent. He did manage to slow their fall and only roll in a heap next to Handrill just as Zonar and the others finished off the huge tarkoza.

"Well done, my little friend. You have shown yourself to have great courage. Roan, I'm very proud of you," Zonar spoke through heaving breaths.

"Now, we must get you three and the girl back to safety. We're vulnerable here where any remaining tarkoza might smell blood," Dentax's voice displayed his concern as he spoke.

Just then two shadows crossed the clearing. It was Jorno flying with Eli on his back, followed by

Galen and Kane. The rescue group descended in haste. Eli's face became pale the moment he saw his precious Roan lying on the ground, wounded. Eli jumped from Jorno's back before the dragon's feet were on the ground.

With shaking hands, Eli encircled Roan's neck in a warm hug. He then focused his attention on Roan's wounds. Opening his first aid pack, Eli applied a salve normally used in the dragon colony to treat mere cuts and abrasions onto Roan's gaping wing wounds. There was nothing he could do here in the forest to repair the damage, only slow the bleeding and prevent infection with the salve. Kane followed Eli's example and began treating the wounds of Handrill and Zonar.

A crashing in the distance brought everyone to attention.

"We leave at once. Our wounds will have to wait until we reach safer ground," Zonar directed. "Galen, you and Kane take the girl. Jorno, I want you and Eli to carry Roan. Can you manage that?"

"Of course, sir, I wouldn't have it any other way," replied Jorno.

Eli assisted Roan in climbing aboard Jorno's back. He then sat facing backwards, with Roan's head in his lap.

Calistor and Dentax flew close to Handrill

and Zonar, offering encouragement as the tired group headed back to the beach.

There was quite a stir on the beach as workers, human and dragon alike, realized the identities of the arriving wounded. Tyffan ran to Eli, eyes filled with fear at the sight of a bloodied Roan. Silence spread across the beach as onlookers watched their fearless dragon king land, chest bloody and scales missing, followed by the wise old Handrill who limped as he set down. Then, the group realized that Kane and Galen brought back another child, safe from the jaws of the tarkoza. A spontaneous cheer rose up for the valiant heroes of the day.

"We rest here before heading back to our own colony," Zonar sighed as he lowered himself to the sand.

~ ~ ~

Back on the Zimley side of the sea the dragon colony was a constant buzz of activity. Zimley's doctors were kept busy treating the wounded Jolarans and dragons who were shuttled across the sea. Tremor supervised all the comings and goings of dragons and people. Marina and Devon proved themselves to be quite adept in caring for wounded dragons and both children worked with the dedication of seasoned dragon-keepers, never

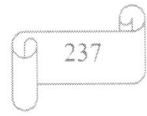

complaining or tiring.

"Look," Devon cried. He was the first to spot the wounded heroes. "Something's wrong with Zonar." Devon felt not only grateful to Zonar for helping the Jolarans, but also a fondness for him because of the kindness which Zonar has shown him upon his arrival at the dragon colony. Devon's mouth gaped and wide eyes filled with tears when he focused his gaze on Zonar's chest wound.

Zonar and Handrill were received by two of the older dragon keepers and a Zimley doctor. Both were quickly ushered into the calm and coolness of the caves where their care was begun immediately. Devon followed, determined to help, tears brimming over onto his cheeks.

"Roan, my beautiful Roan," Marina practically sobbed as she watched Jorno set down carrying Roan on his back.

"He'll be okay," Eli assured her as he coaxed a very weary Roan down.

Together Eli and Marina escorted Roan to his cave, where Eli set about properly treating the little dragon's wounds. Although deep and jagged, the gashes on Roan's wing were treatable. Eli called for a physician to suture the damaged membranes.

"Well, there should be no permanent damage, Eli. The salve you applied in the forest has already begun the healing process. Roan is young and strong. He should heal quickly, though I did have to remove some of the shredded tissue. His wing may be a bit misshapen for the rest of his life. Still, he will be quite able to fly."

"Thanks, Doc." Eli breathed a long sigh of relief knowing that his precious Roan would be fine – eventually.

By nightfall Rosamae had joined her beloved Zonar in their personal cave. The two settled down to enjoy a quiet night curled up together, the first after many long days of battle. Eli settled Roan for the night, knowing that he would wake often to check on Roan's wounds. Marina was beside herself with worry and convinced Eli to let her sleep with Roan also.

Before turning in for the night, Eli walked in silence to the cave entrance. He noticed Jorno walking slowly down the beach. Sprinting to catch up, Eli fell in beside the gentle beast who was fast becoming one of Eli's favorite dragons.

"How much longer do you think this will go on?" Eli asked.

"Until it is finished," Jorno replied with great wisdom.

"So many have been wounded," Eli voiced his thoughts of concern.

"True, but we have lost none in death. For that the colony must be very grateful. The Creator has preserved us all in the face of this dark evil. And we must think about how many Jolaran people we have saved from certain death."

"You're right, Jorno. That makes it all worth it, even Roan's wounds." Eli paused as he gazed at the stars. "We head back into battle in the morning?"

"Together, my friend," Jorno replied with a nod and a twinkle in his eye.

Chapter 30

The Last Tarkoza

After another two weeks, the battles with the tarkoza were far and few between. No further dragons had received serious wounds and the care of survivors on the beach was settling into a consistent daily routine. Food and other needed supplies were flown across the sea every day. Many of the stunned survivors were just beginning to allow themselves to relax a bit. Dentax had been placed in charge of the warriors during Zonar's recovery from his wounds with Galen and Jorno

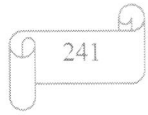

assisting him in battle and supervision.

As Zimzor's twin suns rose above the horizon across the sea to the east, Eli awakened and stretched as he rose from his blanket on the beach. He could see Kane just now waking in the early morning haze. Eli greeted Kane and the two began to set out meat prepared for their dragon friends. Kane enjoyed these brief opportunities to learn from Eli how to care for the gigantic beasts that were so dedicated to saving his people.

Before long, the two friends went to join their parents. A fast friendship was growing between Clarice and Dawson Harcourt and Kane's mother, Anaya. Breakfast was simple: fresh fruit from Zimley's fields and bread flown over the previous evening from the town bakers. Mr. Elliott also ate with the small group as plans for the day were discussed. Dentax, Galen and Jorno joined this core handful of humans.

"Perhaps we've got them all," Mr. Elliott offered hopefully. "We haven't had any major battles for several days now."

"You could be right, I'm just not quite sure," Dawson joined in with his thoughts. "How do we make certain we haven't missed any of those terrible creatures?"

"We can't let the families back into the forest

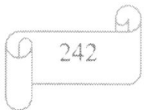

until we're certain – especially the children," came Anaya's soft voice of concern.

"You're right, the children have been so traumatized, I'm not sure how many will ever be comfortable roaming the forest again," Clarice spoke with the wisdom of one who had worked with people who had endured much difficulty in the past.

Galen's deep voice broke into the conversation as the humans mused over the situation. "We must do a careful and thorough search of the entire forest. Only then can we know if it is safe to allow humans to enter the forests and resume their former lives."

"We will devise a search pattern, from the beaches inward, all the way to the mountains." Dentax voiced his plan, a very sensible approach.

"Yes, a search to the mountains. That is the only way," Jorno agreed.

"I concur."

Everyone turned toward the beach at the sound of a voice they hadn't heard in over two weeks.

"Zonar!" Eli shouted as he jumped and ran to hug the huge dragon who had once frightened him so as a novice dragon-keeper.

Zonar's deep, raspy voice chuckled at Eli's

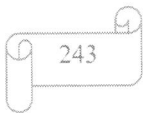

unbridled display of affection. "And do we have a plan for this search?" the refreshed dragon king asked.

Jorno spoke up first. "I think we should begin by lining the beaches as far north and south as possible with dragons and riders. We'll need the warriors, search and rescue teams, and the young messengers all working together."

"Yes and perhaps even some dragons who have served to shuttle supplies across the sea." Zonar agreed with the plan thus far.

"We'll search westward in a tight pattern," Galen added, "Crossing paths often will ensure that no tarkoza are overlooked."

"But we must protect our young messengers. If and when a tarkoza is spotted, the young ones must report to the warriors rather than attack themselves," Jorno interjected. "I don't want to be flying Roan or Celeste or anyone else back for medical care this time."

"Agreed," Zonar's voice boomed. "Dentax, go to our colony now. Summon every able-bodied dragon and keeper. We begin the search as soon as everyone is assembled."

~ ~ ~

Zimzor's suns were high overhead as Zonar flew up and down the beach. A vast array of

dragon scales glistened in a brilliant rainbow the entire length of the beach. Final instructions had been passed up and down the line to humans and dragons alike. Only a minimum of dragons would remain on the beach to protect the Jolaran survivors with Zelina in charge.

"Begin the search," Zonar's thunderous voice boomed.

At once the rainbow of sparkling wings unfurled and the colossal beasts seemed to rise as one dazzling ribbon. Zonar joined the line in the center and led the group up over the cliffs into the forests.

Marina gasped as the wind blew her hair. She and Devon had been recruited as spotters. She watched in amazement, safely strapped in her saddle on Celeste's shoulders, as the enormous group rose aloft. Looking to her right, Marina caught Devon's gaze as he rose aboard Roan. She

waved at the friend she now considered her new brother, and then focused her gaze ahead.

For hours the dragons criss-crossed the forest, diving through dense growth, soaring over rocky outcroppings and coasting down through meadows. Some followed rivers and streams deep into the heart of the forest. It seemed that not a single tarkoza had survived. Had the evil been completely vanquished?

Then, as the evening twilight approached, a terrible and chilling shriek could be heard for miles. Immediately the largest of the warriors descended toward its origin. Zonar, Dentax, Jorno and Galen arrived simultaneously from different directions along with half a dozen other warrior dragons.

There in a small clearing stood an angry tarkoza, slashing its claws at the sky. Handrill and Roan circled overhead, high enough to be clear of those dangerous claws.

"Roan, get your rider to safety," Zonar ordered.

"Yes sir!"

"Now, attack together!"

All ten warriors plunged toward the tarkoza. Mr. Elliott, fired arrows from his perch aboard Handrill, striking the beast in the shoulder. One dragon after another clawed, smacked and slashed at the huge tarkoza. Eli, Kane and Dawson all landed blows from their spears and clubs as their dragons swished down at the tarkoza. The beast fought back furiously, great anger in its screams. But it was hopelessly outnumbered and in only a short time the beast breathed its last and fell to the ground in a bloody heap. The mammoth warriors landed next to their kill to take a few moments to regroup before continuing the search.

"Look where we are," Kane pointed westward as he gazed above.

The group was standing near the tree line on the eastern slopes of the smoking mountains.

"We did it," Elliot's voice filled with amazement. "We've actually followed them all the way to the mountains."

"Caves. Legends have it that they live in caves in these mountains," Kane strained to see any cave entrances as he leaned around Galen's neck.

"Let's complete our search of this side of the forest before nightfall. We'll look for caves in the morning," Zonar's voice was final, though his eyes strained in the same direction that Kane gazed.

Without further conversation, the group ascended, rejoined the search pattern with the others and continued up past the trees to the mountain slopes. Only when all the dragons had

reached the slopes did Zonar call off the search for the night.

Returning to the beach, they shared stories of the one last tarkoza they had eliminated that day. The Jolaran survivors spoke in awe and disbelief that the tarkoza might truly be gone. A collective murmur traveled down the beach as opinions were exchanged in the growing darkness. Then, in exhaustion, dragons and humans lay down together on the beaches of Jolara for a well deserved night's sleep.

Chapter 31

A New Colony

Following a careful search of the mountain slopes, the dragons indeed found caves. Caves large and small. Some of which had obviously been the hibernation homes of the tarkoza. The caves were so numerous that the dragons began to look longingly at such wonderful accommodations in the mountains. They found many caves, but not a single tarkoza. By the end of the day Zonar was ready to declare a complete victory over the deadly beasts.

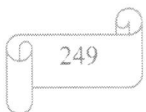

As the final search party returned to the beach, cheers rose from below as dragons, Jolarans and Zimleys celebrated together.

And celebrate they did. Delicious meals were prepared over open fires on the beach. Luscious fresh fruits and vegetables, only the best from Zimley's fields, were flown over for the feast. The Zimley town bakers outdid themselves with the quantity and variety of baked goods created for that one day. Tender meats were roasted over open fire spits. Kane lead any able-bodied Jolaran hunters on a fishing spree, spearing many of the tasty red fleshed fish he had come to savor. Many more of Zimley's townspeople chose to be flown across the sea to join the celebration. Why, even Master Oliver and the town council arrived just prior to the beginning of the feast!

On the beach, extending for a lengthy distance, Jolarans, Zimleys and dragons congregated and mixed together, dined on the delicious feast, sang and danced as afternoon stretched into evening.

With bellies truly full and satisfied for the first time in many weeks, the people settled in small groups along the beach, talking and sharing memories of the long and terrible battles against the evil, blood-thirsty tarkoza.

A loud banging on a kettle slowly quieted the crowd. Heads turned toward the sound.

"Oh no, what does he want?" Kane muttered to Eli.

"Don't know, but I'm sure it will be very officious," snickered Eli.

"A proclamation is in order," Oliver's most official voice echoed across the shore. "Tonight we celebrate a great victory! The victory of our beloved dragons over the terrible beasts from the Jolaran Mountains."

Oliver was interrupted by thunderous cheers from the crowd.

"And now good people, it is time to move on. For our temporary commitment to the people of Jolara is at an end. We, the people of Zimley, must return with our dragon friends to our own coast, never to be disturbed again by the forest people of Jolara."

Boo's and hisses mingled with angry shouts began to swell throughout the crowd.

"What is the meaning of this, Oliver?" Zonar's head snaked down to Oliver's level to look him in the eye.

"Well, we did agree only to help these people through this one crisis and then return to our original peace agreement," Oliver retorted

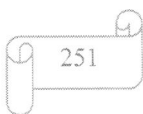

arrogantly.

"Hmm, it seems to me that I distinctly recall telling you that our peace agreement was over," Zonar's eyes sparkled as he toyed with the now defunct leader. "Someone get this worm of a man out of my sight!"

Jorno swooped down and plucked Oliver in his claws muttering *gladly,* then turned toward the sea and winged his way east.

Turning to the crowd Zonar lifted himself to his full, towering height and addressed the crowd.

"Good people of Jolara and Zimley, I propose a new peace agreement. Kane, a young and very brave provider and protector for his small family, risked everything he had. He was willing to lay down his own life to protect them." Zonar paused and met Kane's eyes with an admiring gaze. "I tell you now; no one has greater love than that. Your fellow hunter saw a tremendous and evil danger. Kane sought the truth contained within the ancient Jolaran legends and found hope in the reality those legends revealed. Let Kane be an example to you. Always seek the truth, for only truth can set you free.

"Now, as many of us from the dragon colony have become rather fond of certain Jolarans," he looked from Kane to Anaya and Devon standing

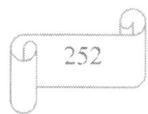

next to Galen, "I suggest that we form a new dragon colony here on the shores of Jolara. Some of your people will be selected to train as dragon-keepers and we, in return, will aid in your forest hunts and protect your people from danger."

The crowd was on their feet in an instant, cheering wildly. Zonar's plan was an immediate success with Jolarans, Zimleys and dragons alike. It took some time before the cheering, dancing, roaring and wing flapping settled down.

"Then we shall camp here for the night and make the necessary arrangements in the morning." With that Zonar returned to his beautiful mate, Rosamae, and stretched out comfortably on the sand to rest.

~ ~ ~

First thing in the morning there were many goodbyes, hugs and tears as Zimley citizens loaded up to return home. Many left supplies and gifts for their new Jolaran friends. Soon dragons were busy flying the first of many trips across the shimmering sea.

Zonar supervised everything from his chosen spot on the cliff above Kane's original cave.

It was to this spot that Eli climbed alone. He respectfully waited for Zonar to acknowledge him before speaking.

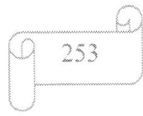

"Sir, I have a request. It is in regards to your plan to form a new colony here on the Jolaran coast. I'd like to volunteer to stay as a dragon-keeper. I could help train Jolarans to care for the dragon colony and I just can't bear the thought of living without my new friends – especially Kane," The words spilled out more quickly than Eli had intended and he found his heart beating rapidly.

Zonar chuckled. "Eli, slow down. Remember you have nothing to fear from me. Now, I remember you and Tyffan were the first among our colony to stand up and help our new friends. Therefore, I think it only fitting for the two of you to be the first keepers offered positions at the new colony." Zonar paused and smiled as he saw Eli visibly relax. "My only concern is with regards to your parents and sister. Can you live so far from them?"

"Maybe we should go ask them."

"Good idea, climb aboard my friend."

Together Eli and Zonar flew down to the beach and landed near the campfire where Eli's family was still enjoying a leisurely discussion with Kane's family. Tyffan, who had worked so closely with Anaya caring for the children and wounded, was there also.

Zonar cleared his throat as a way of entering

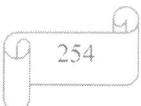

their friendly conversation. "It appears to me we have the beginnings of a new dragon colony – or at least its keepers. My friend, Eli, has volunteered to remain on the Jolaran side of the sea and work with the new colony. Tyffan, I think it is only fitting that you be offered the same opportunity, if you so desire."

Tyffan blushed, and then raised her head toward him.

"Yes, Zonar, I can think of nothing I would like more than to remain here with my new friends."

"Good, good. Mr. and Mrs. Harcourt, how do you feel about your son living so far away? He would not be able to visit you as often as in the past," Zonar bowed his head to the Harcourts as he posed his question.

"Funny you should ask," began Dawson. "We were just discussing the new colony. Clarice and I have decided to remain here with Anaya. She has been a true leader of her people, but she is only one. We would like to offer her our help and friendship forever. That is if Marina can stay here and continue to train as a dragon-keeper for the new colony."

"But Dawson, yours was the only voice of reason on the town council when we needed it most," Zonar's brow wrinkled in concern.

"True, but I think now that Oliver has been ousted there will be many more voices of reason. I feel I could be of greater use here, helping the

Jolarans. Anaya tells me that clan leadership would have fallen to Kane after his father's death. He is brave and I believe he will grow to be a great leader of his people, but they have no one ready to assist in leadership and help make sense of all this destruction."

Anaya smiled at her friends and turned to address Zonar.

"Zonar, I was terrified when I first met you, yet you listened to our plight and helped. I have the greatest respect for you as the dragon king and a deep love for you as a friend. I ask you now to allow my new friends to remain with me. Look how many of our people no longer have families. I can already see that many will band together, forming new families. But there are still many children who have no one. I myself have two new children to look after having taken Maxell and Lissette into my family. Dawson and Clarice are wise and caring. We need their help."

"Lissette? I don't remember anyone by that name." Zonar tipped his head thinking.

Eli smiled and solved the mystery for him, "She's the little girl that Roan saved the day you were both wounded."

"Ah, yes, her I do remember. And how is the child doing?"

"See for yourself." Anaya pointed to a group of children playing at the water's edge. Devon splashed Maxell and Lissette squealed as she ran from his attempts to get her wet.

"So it seems you have some wonderful additions to your family," Zonar's eyes softened in kindness as he watched the children.

"Speaking of children," Mr. Elliott interjected during the lull in conversation. "It seems to me there is a need for a good teacher here. Well over half of the survivors are children and the adults are going to need some extra help with them. I'd like to stay as well."

"What about your job at the school?" Dawson asked.

"Oh, I guess I can send my resignation by way of the dragon patrol."

"Well, then," Zonar inhaled deeply as he spoke. "We have our new colony keepers and human leaders. Between Kane and Anaya, the Harcourts and Professor Elliott, I've no doubt order will be quickly and fairly established among the Jolaran people. Eli and Tyffan will be in charge of the keepers. I'm sure it won't take Kane any time at all to learn the finer points of dragon care. He's already got a good start. I must say, though, that I will miss having Marina in our colony on the

Zimley side. She and I have enjoyed many good afternoon conversations on the rocks. And Devon. Now he's a promising young lad if I do say so. All we need now is to pick the dragons that shall form the new colony."

Golden scales moved in beside Zonar, followed by glistening deep green scales.

"There is no need for you to pick, sir. My mate and I have made our decision. We will be staying here with our friends. I can't really imagine a day without Kane around to talk to or fly with," Galen spoke the thoughts shared by many other dragons.

Jorno and his mate also volunteered for the new colony along with a half dozen other pairs of adult dragons. Zonar agreed that both Eli and Tyffan's training groups of young dragons should remain with their keepers. Besides, the young dragons, especially Roan and Celeste, had proven themselves valuable in the fight to save the Jolarans. They deserved the honor. It was decided that Galen and Jorno would share in leadership of the new colony for the time being. Dentax considered remaining with the new colony, though his duties on the dragon council were considerable and his leadership would be needed as the new peace agreement was put into place with the Zimleys.

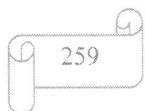

"I guess that settles things. The rest of us will be heading back soon," Zonar said with a note of finality.

"Now you just wait one minute, Zonar!"

Everyone turned; stunned that anyone would address Zonar in such a tone. It was none other than the usually timid, compliant and smiling Zelina, not wanting to be forgotten.

"You forgot to ask me where I wanted to live and serve," Zelina's eyes danced as she addressed the leader.

Sharing her sense of humor, Zonar smiled and bowed as she approached.

"My dear friend, how neglectful of me! Please forgive my indiscretion. And where would your heart's desire be? To live in this new colony or back at our home on the Zimley shore?"

"I may be on old dragon. And I've seen my days supervising new keepers and young ones. But I've still got a spirit of adventure and my heart lies here, rebuilding the lives of these lovely people," Zelina savored her moment as she replied.

"Then here you shall stay. Although, I don't know how we will manage without you in our colony," Zonar chuckled and winked at her.

And so the day progressed as the remaining Zimley citizens and dragons left for the Zimley shore. Zonar and Rosamae were the last to leave. The kind and wise dragon king circled the group of dragons and people on the beach, tipped his wings to the many waves from below and soared out across the sea, leaving below a very happy group. More than a new colony really – close friends; family forever.

Mary Harrison

About the Author

Mary Harrison lives in Florida where she works as an artist, author and educator. Harrison earned her MFA from the Academy of Art University and uses her art to create stunning, full color paintings that enhance written imagery, encouraging readers' imaginations and desire to read on and on. *The Dragons of Zimzor* is her debut novel.

Prints from the original full color paintings in this book are available for order at the artist's website: www.maryharrisonfineart.weebly.com

Made in the USA
Lexington, KY
26 January 2012